THE NINE NAUGHTY NOVELISTS

presents

Nine Nights in New Orleans:

9 short stories

ISBN
978-0-9838840-4-0

Kindle Edition
Copyright 2014

Published by Nine Naughty Novelists

Foreword

Once upon a time, there were nine naughty novelists. They were from all over the United States and Canada, and through the magic of the Internet, they came together for blog hijinks, friendship, and more. They bonded over their shared love of wine, chocolate, shoes, and good books. But they had never been in the same place at once.

Until one lucky weekend in New Orleans.

There was much walking and sightseeing. There were beignets and hurricanes and Voodoo shops. Plans were made and projects were started. Copious amounts of writing occurred. Amazing food was consumed. Much laughter filled the air. There may have been wine involved.

Okay, there may have been a *lot* of wine involved.

Somewhere during the work and play and fun, they decided they needed to write about New Orleans. "It'll be fun! We should all include three secret words! Let's call it Nine Nights in New Orleans!"

And so it happened.

Welcome to our tribute to friendship, romantic fiction, and New Orleans!

Juniper Bell   Kelly Jamieson
Meg Benjamin   Skylar Kade
P.G. Forte   Erin Nicholas
Kate Davies   Sydney Somers
Kinsey Holley

CONTENTS

Ash Wednesday *by Meg Benjamin*

Maggie Beaulieu got out of the cab at Magazine and Canal. For the fifth time, she checked to make sure she had the tote bag. Last night, she dreamed she'd left it at a 7-Eleven near the airport by accident.

Wish fulfillment Maggie?

No. Definitely not. This might not be the most pleasant task she'd ever undertaken, but she'd do it and she'd do it right. Uncle Claude was depending on her to take care of things. He'd chosen her over all the other cousins. She'd show him he'd made the right decision.

Not that any of the other cousins had been all that eager to do it. On the other hand, they hadn't been all that enthusiastic about Maggie doing it either.

You sure about this, honey? It's a lot of responsibility. Don't you think maybe we should do something a little more normal?

Maggie sighed. She'd have loved normal herself, but that wasn't what she'd been asked to do. No, if Uncle Claude wanted normal, he would have said he wanted normal. Instead, he'd said he wanted Maggie. She took a deep breath and blew it out, probably the first of many deep breaths she'd be taking over the course of the evening. With any luck, after tonight, everyone else would agree that Claude had made the right decision after all. Or if not exactly the right decision, at least not the wrong one.

She started a brisk stroll down Decatur Street, doing her best to look like someone just out for an evening's walk along the riverside. If nothing else, maybe after she'd done what she'd set out to do she could go to the French Market for a couple of beignets and coffee.

1

Oh yeah, Maggie. Let's pretend this is just like any other delivery. Maybe you could go over to Royal and have a hurricane.

She hugged the tote bag closer to her side. Okay, so maybe this evening's adventure wasn't typical. But she'd try to behave as if it were. Couples walked past her arm in arm, most of them smiling blissfully. Music echoed from some of the clubs, saxophones and guitars. A humid breeze slid over her cheek, smelling faintly of decay and the river.

The river. Time to move toward the riverside.

A group of women careened up the street, tottering on stiletto heels, their pastel sun dresses slightly wilted from the heat. Three of them had stacks of multi-colored metallic beads around their necks. The fourth wore a plastic crown with the number thirty at the peak. All of them carried paper cups.

Maggie detoured around them a little wistfully. She'd love to have a birthday party in New Orleans herself, tottering through the French Market with a glass of Voodoo Juice. Actually, she'd love to be doing just about anything other than what she was actually doing.

You could have said no. Nobody would have blamed you.

They wouldn't have blamed her, but they wouldn't have done it themselves either. And somebody had to do it. They owed it to Uncle Claude.

She did the deep breath thing again. Time to move on. It wasn't like she had all night.

She headed up St. Louis toward Woldenberg Park. She sort of remembered walking along the sidewalk above the river there with her mother. Not that they'd ever gotten close to the water, even when they went to the park. She'd have to try to figure out her strategy once she got down there.

She sighed again. "Listen, Uncle Claude," she murmured. "I really do appreciate your having faith in me and all, but are you absolutely sure you wouldn't like to just go back to Houston?"

Derek Bartel stuffed the collection of coins and folding money into his pocket before sliding his fiddle back into the velvet-lined case. The money wasn't as much as he'd hoped, but it wasn't bad for a weeknight.

Around him, tourists still strolled across Jackson Square, pausing to take pictures in front of St. Louis Cathedral. The metal-painted man who imitated statues stood frozen in place as a pair of children giggled in front of him.

Dolan had found a prime spot for their trio tonight on Chartres. People walking by could pause to listen for a few minutes before moving on, hopefully after dropping a couple of bucks into Derek's fiddle case.

Dolan, the keyboard man, was breaking down his equipment. He'd already split the take from Derek's case, probably raking off a little extra for himself when he did it. But since Dolan was the one who organized the group and found the spot for them to set up, Derek figured he deserved a little more for his trouble.

The bass guitarist, Peebo, didn't feel the same way. "C'mon man, hand it over. I got rent to pay, same as you."

Dolan grimaced, then handed him another couple of bills. "Take was thin tonight."

Peebo shrugged. "Better than nothing." He hoisted his case to his shoulder and turned up Chartres. "Later, dudes."

Derek picked up his own case, watching Dolan fold up the tablecloth he'd spread in front of them to catch any overflow from the donations. "We doing this again tomorrow?"

Dolan shrugged. "Could be. Come on down anyway. If Peebo don't show up, you and me can try doing some stuff on our own."

Which meant he probably wouldn't pass the news on to Peebo. Looked like they were about to become a duet. *Oh well.* Derek didn't like confrontations. He wasn't somebody who sought out trouble. He thought of himself mostly as a live and let live type. Mostly. "Good enough."

He tucked his case under his arm and headed down St. Peter toward the river. It was a fair hike to his apartment, but the evening was clear and fairly cool, and walking saved bus fare. He only used his car for trips outside the city these days, whenever he could pick up a gig. Good for the environment. Also good for his own chronically thin wallet.

The street lights cast glowing pools along the sidewalk, leaving shadows in the doorways of the closed shops and cafés. He could still hear music from the clubs along Decatur, soft echoes of saxophones and guitars.

A block away, the cast iron lamps of the Moonwalk and Woldenberg Park glowed enticingly. Great place to go strolling with somebody, as several couples seemed to have discovered that evening. On an impulse, he crossed the street and climbed the steps to the raised walkway along the riverside. Might as well enjoy the cool evening air as long as he could.

Ahead of him, he saw another solo walker, female, carrying a canvas tote at her side. She wandered slowly along the river, gazing out across the water, her dark hair catching reflected gleams as she passed the light posts. Something about her made him pause.

So slow. So sad. Just like Juliette.

He closed his eyes for a moment. He hadn't thought about Juliette in years—it wasn't like she was always on his mind. Still, now that he had thought of her, he started watching the woman with the tote bag a little more carefully. He slowed his own steps to stay behind her, hoping she wouldn't decide he was a particularly inept mugger. She seemed to be looking down at the dark river water beyond the high bank, her steps slowing even more, her shoulders rounding with fatigue.

Don't bother her. Not every sad person is looking to hurt herself. Live and let live, remember?

But even saying that to himself started a train of thought he couldn't seem to stop. *What if she's looking for a good place to jump, a place where no one will see her?* The thought drifted through his mind as she paused for a moment, gazing toward the far bank. Maybe a place like the very spot where she was currently standing. *And if she decides to do something like jump, I'm the only one here. I'm the only one who can talk her out of it.*

Well, crap.

Maggie gazed across the river toward the far shore. Somehow her childhood memory of the place was very different. She'd remembered a high wall with the water directly below, absolutely perfect for her purposes. Instead, a grassy bank sloped down to a heap of stones stretching along the water's edge. Anything dropped from the walk would land on grass or stones rather than in the river.

She grimaced in frustration. *Damn it, this was supposed to be so simple. Walk along the river and just get it done, easy peasy.* Instead she was going to have to find something like a bridge that could take her out over the water. Only all the bridges she could see were strictly for cars. If she walked out on one of them, she'd probably end up squashed flat under somebody's SUV.

Lake Pontchartrain might be easier, but it wouldn't satisfy Uncle Claude. He'd said the Mississippi, and he meant the Mississippi. Now that she'd come all the way here from Texas, she wasn't about to take the easy way out—if she'd wanted to do that, she could have stayed home in the first place.

She stepped back from the edge of the walk and felt a quick stab of uneasiness. A man was watching her a little way down the sidewalk. He carried something, and she strained to see what it was in the dim illumination from the street lights along the walk.

Looked like an instrument case of some kind, maybe a violin. Her shoulders relaxed. Nobody who played a violin could be threatening, could he? Unless he was actually hiding weapons in the case, like some Philharmonic Jack the Ripper or something.

Letting your imagination go a little crazy, right Maggie?

The man took a cautious step closer. "Good evening," he said. "Nice night."

Maggie nodded carefully. "Yes, it is."

"Are you looking for someplace in particular? I live around here—I might be able to help."

He looked a little like a poet, although Maggie wasn't sure she'd have thought that if he hadn't been carrying the violin case. His hair curled over the top of his collar, brushing his eyebrows in front. She couldn't be sure of the color in the dim light, but it looked reddish brown.

Brown eyes too, as far as she could tell. Tall. Slender. Long tapering fingers that were probably really good for playing the violin.

And other things.

Stop that. It wasn't like she was here for a relationship. She had Uncle Claude to think about.

"I'm just taking a walk," she explained. "I'm not going anywhere special."

"Oh." He looked a little worried all of a sudden. "Do you mind if I walk with you, then? I live in this direction."

She shrugged, narrowing her eyes. That seemed like an innocent enough request. "Well, sure, I guess that would be all right."

He stuck out the hand that wasn't holding the violin case. "I'm Derek Bartel."

"Maggie Beaulieu." She gave his hand a quick shake, shifting the tote bag a little to do it. "You're from New Orleans?"

He shrugged. "I live here now. I'm from Memphis originally."

Maggie began walking again, keeping an eye on the river bank. Maybe the stones didn't go all the way along the shore. Maybe she'd get lucky and find a bare spot where she could walk down to the edge.

"Where are you from?" Derek Bartel stepped between her and the river bank, neatly blocking her view.

"Houston," she snapped, and then regretted it. He was just being nice after all. "Could I move on the other side of you? I like to see the river in the moonlight."

"Oh." He paused. "Well…sure. If you want to, I guess."

Maggie frowned. She didn't see why wanting to have a view of the river should be such a big deal. "Thanks."

He gave her a quick smile. "So you're visiting?"

"In a way. My family used to live here—a while ago." It seemed a lot longer now that she thought about it. Everything looked different from the way she remembered.

She bit her lip. She'd promised, damn it. And now it looked like it wasn't going to work. At least not here. She'd have to find another way to get out on the water. Maybe in daylight. Maybe...

She closed her eyes for a moment. She was going to mess it up. Just like everybody thought she would. Everybody except Uncle Claude.

Do not cry. Do not cry in front of a stranger.

"I guess that can be sort of...melancholy." Derek Bartel's voice was soft. "Coming back to where you used to live when you don't live here anymore. Some of the memories can be sort of sad."

Maggie blinked. She hadn't really thought of it that way. Was she just feeling so down because things had changed? "I guess it can."

She began walking again, slowly, looking out at the river below. If she stood on the top of the bank, it looked like the water came closer to the edge here. Maybe she could get near enough to deal with Uncle Claude.

"And the other thing is, night can make things seem worse sometimes." Derek was talking a little more quickly now. "Problems can seem more serious at night for some reason."

"I guess." Maggie wasn't really listening to him. She was trying to figure out how she could get down to the river from here without breaking her neck—she should have brought a flashlight. And possibly better shoes.

"Look, Maggie." Derek stepped in front of her. "The thing is, I mean what I'm trying to say is you shouldn't do anything rash right now. Whatever it is that's troubling you, you can work on it tomorrow. It's not like you have to do something right this minute. Think about it first. Just think."

Maggie narrowed her eyes. Did he know about Uncle Claude, was he some kind of river cop? *Okay, reality check Maggie.* Of course he didn't. And river cops wouldn't go around carrying violins. But in that case, what the hell was he talking about?

"Please. Just think." His eyes were definitely brown. Sort of like chocolate. "Don't do anything you can't undo."

"Okay," she said slowly. "What was it I was supposed to think about?"

"Just don't do anything rash." He took a deep breath. "Don't hurt yourself, okay? Whatever it was that happened. It's not worth hurting yourself. I'll stay here with you and talk if that will help."

Maggie narrowed her eyes. *What the hell?* "You'll stay here with me?"

He nodded. "Sure. All night if you want. I've got nothing I have to do right now."

Don't hurt yourself. It took her another long moment, but the penny finally dropped. "You think I'm trying to commit suicide?"

For the first time he looked a little uncertain. "Well…yeah. Or just, you know, that you were upset. I know what it feels like to be desperate. I've been there."

She stared out at the water for a long moment. "If I told you I was perfectly okay, would you go on about your business and leave me alone here?"

Should have stayed out of it, Bartel. Should have just gone on home.

Except, of course, he couldn't do that. His memories of Juliette wouldn't let him.

He glanced at the oversized tote bag she held tightly against her side. "I might. How about if we make a deal here. You show me what's in your tote bag, and I go off and leave you to whatever the hell it is you want to do."

"My tote bag?" Her eyes widened and she hugged the bag closer to her chest. "Why would I show you what's inside my tote bag? Why the hell should I?"

He sighed. "Look, I had this friend once who got really depressed after she broke up with her boyfriend. We were close, or I thought we were, anyway. She tried to kill herself. I felt guilty afterward because I didn't realize how upset she was, and I didn't try to help her."

Maggie frowned. "What did she do?"

He grimaced. They were getting off track here. "She jumped into the school fish pond. She didn't drown, but she got really wet and she killed a bunch of fish."

Her frown stayed in place. "Oh. Well. That's good, isn't it?"

Derek sighed. *Really off track.* "It was good that she didn't drown, but she ended up barfing all over the landscaping. It caused a big stink. Literally. Her parents had to take her out of school—I never saw her again after that."

Maggie's lips were trembling, but he guessed she was trying not to laugh. Why didn't anybody ever take this as seriously as he had? Too bad Juliette had tried to kill herself so dramatically—and failed so spectacularly. "Hey, it may have been stupid, but I still felt bad about it. I mean

I missed what she was feeling. Completely. And she was my friend. I saw you up here tonight and you looked so sad. I just couldn't…" He took a deep breath. "Look, just show me what's in the bag, so I know it's not a Glock or something, okay? I promise I'll leave you alone after that."

She watched him for a moment longer, then shrugged. "Okay, you asked for it." She set the tote bag on the ground and reached inside, pulling out a bright pink quilted bag and a leather clutch. "My purse and my toothbrush and stuff in case I needed to stay over, which it looks like I will." She reached in again and pulled out another handful of miscellaneous stuff. "Change of clothes, paperback, cell phone." She reached in one more time, and pulled out a metal box around six inches by six inches. "And Uncle Claude."

Derek narrowed his eyes. *Okay, this is new.* "Uncle Claude?"

She shrugged again. "He was actually my great uncle, but everybody called him Uncle Claude because it was easier. He moved to Houston when the rest of my family did, but he lived here in New Orleans for most of his life."

Derek stared hard at the box. "And now?"

"He died about a month ago. These are his ashes."

Derek blew out a long breath. "And you carry them around with you now so you can remember him?"

She shook her head. "Good lord, no! That would be sort of demented, right?"

"Yeah, I'd say so." He rubbed a hand across his chin. "But then why do you have them with you?"

She sighed, dropping the metal box back in the bag as she leaned down to pick up her possessions. "I have them because Uncle Claude believed in me."

Derek Bartel was really a very nice man, Maggie decided. Having pressured her into revealing the contents of her tote bag, he now helped her pile everything back in.

He picked up her paperback from the pavement and then handed it to her. "This Uncle Claude thing sounds like a long story."

She shook her head. "Nope. It's actually pretty straightforward. I'm sort of the family screw-up. You give me something to do and like as not I'll get it wrong." She grimaced, remembering that time when she'd taken Aunt Tootie's Pekingese in for grooming, or that time she was supposed to pick up Cousin Rhonda's Cadillac from the mechanic, or the infamous incident when she'd tried to clean her mother's antique cast-iron skillet. None of them had been her fault exactly. On the other hand, they were sort of typical of what seemed to happen to her more often than not. "I always give it my best shot, but I don't always hit the target exactly right."

"But your Uncle Claude thought you could do better?"

She nodded. "He did. He always told me I had it in me. He thought I just had a run of bad luck. Of course that run has lasted for ten or twelve years, but bless him for thinking so."

Derek sat down on a nearby park bench, patting the seat beside him in invitation. "So what are you supposed to be doing with his ashes?"

She sank down beside him. "Well, I told you Uncle Claude came from here, right?"

He nodded. "Right."

"He moved to Houston when my mom and dad did so he could be close to family. He lived in a retirement home there."

12

He nodded again, smiling in a sort of *keep going* way.

She turned and looked back across the river again. Maybe the lights were Algiers. She remembered her mom talking about Algiers. "So Uncle Claude always wanted to come back here. He really missed it. He used to tell me stories about New Orleans, about what it was like to live here since I didn't remember it all that well."

Derek tipped his head back. "Okay. I think I see where this is going."

"Right, well when he died, he had it in his will that his ashes should be scattered in the Mississippi in New Orleans. And that I should do the scattering."

"Why did he want you to do it?"

She sighed. "Like I said, he believed in me. I think he felt like if I came to New Orleans and scattered his ashes myself, I'd have accomplished something. And I'd see New Orleans to boot. Besides, none of the other cousins wanted to do it. Might as well be me."

"Okay." He blew out a breath. "So you're looking for a place to do the scattering?"

"I am." She looked around the park again, managing not to sigh this time. "Only I didn't remember that there were all those rocks along the river side. I mean, I thought I could just come to the park and dump the ashes from up here."

He frowned. "No, you'll definitely have to get down closer to the water. And there's a fence between here and there."

"I noticed." This time she did sigh. "If I could just get down to the bottom of the slope, I think I could do it. Maybe climb out on the rocks and then dump the ashes in the water. Looks like the current would carry them away. Maybe I could climb over that fence."

Derek turned and looked again at the railing that ran along the sidewalk, which was probably meant to keep visitors from doing just what she was planning to do. After a moment, he shrugged. "It's not that high."

She nodded. "It's not."

"I could give you a boost."

She glanced at him, trying to see if he was serious. He was. "Okay."

"We'll need to hide our stuff before we try it, though. I don't want my fiddle to end up in the water." He tucked his violin case under the bench where it was more or less hidden in the shadows.

Maggie pulled the metal box out of her tote bag, then stowed the bag next to his violin case. "What now?"

"Now we figure out exactly where would be the best spot to do this."

"I've sort of figured that out already," she said quickly. "There's a break in the rocks a little way down from here."

She walked to the railing, balancing Uncle Claude against her hip.

"Ready?" He raised an eyebrow.

She nodded.

He placed his hands on her waist and lifted her to the top of the railing.

Maggie caught her breath. She'd been expecting him to just give her foot a boost so that she could step up. But she managed to hover for a moment on the top of the railing and then jump to the other side.

In another moment, Derek leapt over the railing to join her. "Where's this break in the stones?"

She pointed toward the river's edge, trying to get her breath. She could still feel the warmth of his hands at her waist.

"Okay. Looks like we'll need to sort of slide down the bank and then climb out on the rocks. Are you ready?"

She nodded, pulling off her sandals and tucking them beneath the railing. They'd been great for walking in the park, but she had a feeling trying to wear them while climbing on the rocks would earn her a quick dip in the Mississippi, probably with a broken neck.

Derek took her hand, then led her in a sort of half-walk half-slide down the grassy bank to the edge of the rock pile.

What the hell are you doing? You said you'd leave her alone if she unpacked the tote. Yes, he had said that. But he was here anyway. There was just something about Maggie Beaulieu—those soulful eyes, that slightly tousled look about the hair—that made his protective sense go into overdrive. Not that she acted like she needed protection. Right now she was studying the river bank with slightly narrowed eyes.

"Maybe there?"

"Maybe." He took her hand again, heading toward the edge of the rocks. He thought he could see a narrow channel between a couple of small boulders leading out to a large, flat rock at the end. He started forward carefully, trying to avoid sharp pebbles and bits of glass. Why she'd decided to go barefoot he wasn't sure, but he'd just as soon she didn't end up in the emergency room getting stitches. The moon shone dimly overhead. He could barely see the surface of the rocks they were clambering across. The possibility of Maggie tottering out to the edge with her metal box seemed less and less realistic.

"I could go out there for you," he said quietly. "I've got boots on."

She glanced down at his motorcycle boots, doubtfully.

"If you give me your Uncle Claude, I could dump him out there at the end." Always assuming he didn't go into the river with the ashes.

She seemed to consider the idea for a long moment. But then she sighed. "No. It has to be me. He wanted me to do it."

He took a moment to mentally damn Uncle Claude, then shrugged. "Okay. Let's try it."

The next twenty minutes were definitely not a time he wanted to remember later. He managed to move in front of her, feeling his way tentatively between the boulders. She slipped along after him, sometimes grabbing hold of his hip for balance.

Of course, having her hand on his hip didn't do much for his own balance.

Finally, they reached a large flat rock near the edge of the water. "This is as far as we can go. It's too dark to see the rest of the rocks in the water well enough to climb over them. I'm afraid we'll both end up in the river if we try it."

She stepped beside him, trying to see the water in the darkness. "How close are we?"

"About a yard or so that way." He pointed toward the dark river, lapping gently at the edge of the rocks.

She shook her head. "I don't know if I can get the ashes into the water if I'm standing here. There's too much rock in the way."

He managed not to grit his teeth. *You chose to be here, Bartel.* "I can hold your hand while you lean out— that's about the best I can do."

She licked her lips. The dark water sloshed against the rocks a few feet away. "Okay, let's try it."

He helped her climb onto a rock with a sort of round surface where she could balance, carefully wedging his own feet so that he could hold her steady.

She picked up Uncle Claude, wiggling the lid in her hand as she worked it loose. Then she set it on the rocks next to her feet. "Okay. I'm ready."

He stepped forward, bracing one foot again, then took hold of her hand. "Grab my wrist, and I'll grab hold of yours. We'll be stronger that way."

She took hold of his wrist, then leaned out as far as she could, holding one end of the box. "This is it," she muttered, and gave the box a shake.

It would have worked. Derek was almost certain of that. If only a puff of breeze hadn't come up at just that moment. Most of the ashes poured into the water, but a small cloud of Uncle Claude's remains blew back toward Maggie.

For a moment, he thought she'd be okay, but then she squeaked, jumping backward and dropping the box at the same time. He heard it strike the rocks and then slide clattering into the water, just as her feet began to slip out from under her.

She squeaked again, much louder this time, swinging her free hand desperately to try to regain her balance, and suddenly let go of his hand. Her arms windmilled as she began to topple toward the river with agonizing slowness.

He lunged forward, wrapping his arms around her waist then lifting her up and back as they both collapsed onto the rocks.

Or rather, Derek was on the rocks. With one more very loud squeak, Maggie collapsed onto Derek, managing to lodge her elbow somewhere around his diaphragm as she did.

17

"Are you okay?" she stammered.

"Mmmph." Her hair was in his mouth, making it that much more difficult to get back the breath he'd just lost. She moved her head so that he was no longer inhaling her hair. "Derek?"

"I'm okay," he wheezed. "Mostly. I think."

"Hey, you, down there. What the hell is going on?"

The light that shone on them was so bright he was dazzled for a moment. Maggie scrambled to the side. Derek managed to push himself semi-upright, one arm anchored around her waist to keep her from sliding off into the water.

"I said, what the hell is going on down there?"

The light moved slightly, and he got a look at the man in uniform holding the spotlight. He thought the guy was a cop, but he wasn't entirely sure—he might be private security. Still, he looked sort of official. "Just taking in some evening air, officer." He tried for a friendly smile, but the wheezing kind of undercut it.

The light moved to the side, landing on Maggie. "You okay, miss?" the cop called. "You need any assistance?"

She stared back at him wide-eyed. "Why, I'm perfectly fine," she trilled. "It's such a nice night."

The cop didn't look convinced. Derek wasn't surprised. "You're sure?"

"I'm absolutely positive," she said. She turned to Derek, cupping his face in her hands, and pressing her lips to his.

He wasn't exactly ready for her, but that didn't prove to be a problem. His arms went around her waist almost automatically and he angled his head to deepen the kiss. Her mouth opened beneath his and he slid his tongue across hers, feeling a sudden charge of heat that

18

sent the pain rocketing from his diaphragm to his groin. He moved his hand up her spine, feeling warm smooth skin and silken hair beneath his palm.

He slid his fingers into her hair, moving his mouth against hers, as heat raced through his body. He heard her soft sigh somewhere in the back of his brain. He leaned further, bending her body against his arm.

After a moment, she pulled back, blinking at him. Then she brought her fingers to her lips. He didn't blame her—his own lips felt like they were on fire.

What was that? What the hell was that?

"Okay then," the cop called. "Y'all need to come up out of there now. Nobody's supposed to be down on those rocks at night. Not safe."

"Yes sir," Derek croaked, his gaze locked on hers. "We'll do that right now." *As soon as I feel like I can start breathing again.*

"Sorry," Maggie whispered. "I'm sorry. It seemed like a good idea at the time."

He tried to come up with something witty and nonchalant, but his mind immediately went blank. All he could do was nod.

"I guess we'd better climb back up." She chewed on her full lower lip, much fuller than the upper one. *Bee-stung lips.* He wasn't sure where that came from. He hadn't even remembered those words up to now.

Steady. "I guess we'd better." He extended a hand to her, helping her to her feet as he once again tried for nonchalance and once again failed completely. "Up we go."

"Yeah." She sighed. "Let's do that."

The climb back up was a little harder than the one down had been. The grass was slick, and Maggie managed to step on a couple of sharp pebbles before she got all the way to the top. Derek climbed silently beside her, keeping his attention carefully on the railing above them.

She felt a little like kicking herself, which was the way she felt a lot of the time. *Why did you kiss him, idiot? You could just as easily have grabbed his hand or something. The cop just needed to see you weren't being held against your will.*

On the other hand, that had been quite some kiss. She couldn't regret it all that much.

Once they reached the railing, he hopped over, then turned and extended his hand to help her back to the sidewalk. For just a moment, they stood side by side. Then he moved to the park bench, bending down to retrieve his fiddle case.

Maggie dropped onto the bench, holding her sandals in one hand. Now she'd have to find herself a hotel room somewhere. It was way too late to try to get a flight home.

She closed her eyes. She hadn't exactly done Uncle Claude proud. Yes, she'd scattered the ashes in the Mississippi, along with the box they'd come in. But she'd always pictured the process as being a little more dignified than that, particularly since she'd ended up flattening the person who'd tried to help her. *Par for the course, Maggie. Par for the course.*

But still, she'd done it. Uncle Claude was well and truly launched.

She leaned her head back against the bench again, feeling the evening breeze brush across her face. *So long, Uncle Claude. Love you.*

All of a sudden, she heard the sound of a violin, slow and pure, "Amazing grace, how sweet the sound…"

She opened her eyes. Derek stood next to the bench, his open case at his feet. He stared out at the river, coaxing the hymn from his fiddle. Her heart seemed to contract, as her eyes filled. Just the kind of send-off Uncle Claude would have wanted. Her lips moved silently, mouthing the words to the lovely, tremulous notes.

She waited until the last sound floated across the night air, then rubbed the tears away from her cheeks. Stupid and half-assed as her efforts might have been, they'd worked in the end. She'd come to New Orleans and done what she'd set out to do.

Derek loosened his bow and slid it into the top of his case, then put the violin reverently into its place.

"Thank you," she whispered.

He nodded. "You're welcome."

She reached beneath the bench for her tote bag, then stood, trying to remember the way back to Canal.

"Hey?" he said.

She looked back. "Yes?"

"Would you like to get a cup of coffee with me? Maybe some pastry?"

She took a deep breath, then blew it out. The last of the evening. "Yes sir, I would. I'd like that fine."

His lips curved up slowly. "And for the record, the kiss was a good idea. At the time. At any time."

Her heart gave a quick flutter as she slung the tote bag over her shoulder. "I don't suppose you could recommend a good hotel around here. Looks like I'll be spending the night."

His grin broadened. "We can discuss it. Over coffee."

She gave him a grin of her own. "Oh my, I do love New Orleans."

He draped his arm around her shoulders, guiding her toward the stairs. "And New Orleans loves you right back, darlin'. Believe me, right back."

Blame It on the Voodoo *by PG Forte*

"It's getting to where you can't swing a dead chicken around here anymore without it smacking into one damn psychic or another."

Zirondelle Doucette couldn't help the grin that spread across her face as she listened to her Aunt Serafina's complaints. Her aunt stood at the window of their family's shop, staring out at the street, and Zee didn't have to guess too hard to figure out the cause for her discontent. Another "damn" psychic had recently put out her shingle in the previously vacant storefront directly across from their own.

"And if it's not a psychic it's a card reader," the other woman continued, grumbling crossly. "Or a palm reader. Or tea-leaf reader—"

"Or a purveyor of Voodoo essentials?" Zee suggested, holding up the little gris-gris bag she'd just finished assembling.

Serafina turned her head to glare at her niece. "Don't sass me, Zee. You know exactly what I'm talking about."

"Yes, Ma'am, I do." Ducking her head, Zee started in on the next charm. She knew it wasn't psychics per se with whom her aunt had a problem. Serafina was a tolerant soul, not the kind who'd ever take a stand against anyone else's religion or spellcraft or spiritual beliefs. It was the idea of all those make-believe mystics making a mockery of their family's calling that was trying the older woman's temper, and not without cause. The Doucette family had owned and operated their establishment in the self-same Royal Street location for several generations, dealing in authentic rituals, in candles and jujus, talismans and spells. It was hard not to take it personally when your way of life was turned into a kind of circus act by greedy imposters. But as Zee and her aunt both knew, the charlatans did in fact have a place and a purpose in the grand scheme of things.

Oh, how the tourists loved them. They ate up their acts and purchased their trinkets as eagerly as they did the beignets at the Café du Monde. Or jazz on Frenchmen Street. Or hurricanes in Pat O's Courtyard. It was all part of the Crescent City mystique, like Po' Boys and crawfish, pralines and beads. In an odd way, they kept things safe. They kept the merely curious from straying into dangerous territory.

"Oh, Lawd." Aunt Serafina's sudden gasp caught Zee's attention. She glanced up in surprise.

"Auntie, what's wrong?"

"It's him." Serafina scurried back behind the counter where her niece was working, babbling nonsensically. "He's back. He's coming this way. What should we do? What does he want this time?"

"Do about what?" Zee asked, feeling mystified and mildly exasperated. "Who's back?" She loved Serafina; truly she did. Her aunt had taken Zee in after her parents passed, without question or hesitation—the only member of their somewhat eccentric family who seemed to have any idea about what to do with a bewildered little girl who'd suddenly been orphaned. Zee would never forget the older woman's kindness but, all the same, there were times, like now, when dealing with her aunt seriously tried Zee's patience.

The Doucette family had a certain reputation; they were known for being fierce and fearless. They prided themselves on it, in fact. But Serafina had always been unusually timid for a Doucette. Right now, her pale eyes, also unusual in a Doucette, were wide with fear, the pupils dilated; her voice was but a whisper. "Monsieur Boudreaux."

Boudreaux. The name itself meant very little. It was as common as dishwater around those parts. But between the look on her aunt's face and the singing certainty in her own heart, Zee knew exactly which Monsieur Boudreaux Serafina meant. She meant Rene Alcide Boudreaux. Zirondelle's Monsieur Boudreaux. Dominant. Vampire. Master.

But not her master. No, not yet.

As the door to the shop swung open, Zee trembled inside. She couldn't even raise her eyes to gaze upon the shadow that she knew must be filling the entryway. Odd, considering that shadow contained the very thing for which she'd been longing.

"Good evening, Madame Doucette, Mademoiselle." Rene glided into the shop with his usual preternatural grace. He had a way of moving that Zee found mesmerizing. And his voice! That subtle growl, as dark and seductive as midnight, left Zee wanting to fall to her knees at his feet and declare her submission right then and there. She dared not, however. Not with her aunt looking on. Not when she hadn't yet been granted the right.

"Monsieur Boudreaux." Serafina's voice shook a little as she returned his greeting. "What a surprise. We weren't expecting you."

"Weren't you?"

"Well, yes. I mean…no! It—it's so soon after Monsieur's last visit."

That was sadly true, Zee reflected. Although he'd once been a regular customer, stopping by every few weeks, things had changed in the last decade. Nowadays it was not unusual for a year or more to pass between encounters. Rene's last visit to the shop had been three months ago. The occasion was burned into Zee's memory because it was then she decided that enough was enough. It was time to take matters into her own hands, to go after what she wanted, to stop waiting, hoping or dreaming that Rene might someday recall her existence. She could be dead by the time that happened!

"Indeed," Rene agreed. "However, I'm sure you'll appreciate that circumstances have made it necessary that I return sooner rather than later. I'm here because of the spell that's been placed upon me—the curse, if you will."

"A curse!" Serafina gasped in alarm. "Oh, surely Monsieur is mistaken."

"I assure you, Madame, the mistake is not mine. It would, in fact, be rather impossible for me to be mistaken about such a thing. You see, if there's one thing we vampires are very familiar with, it's curses. Centuries of people wishing one dead or ill tends to naturally have that effect."

"But...who would dare do such a thing?"

Zee glanced at her aunt in surprise. Any number of people, she was tempted to reply. Was that not the very reason Rene had been coming to them all these years? He'd been their most loyal customer since practically the first day they'd opened for business. The Doucettes had grown rich selling charms and protection spells to people like Rene Boudreaux. Even if she privately shared her aunt's skepticism, surely it was bad business to mention the fact!

Rene's brow furrowed. He stared searchingly at Serafina for several seconds, then inclined his head. "I apologize. I'm sorry to have alarmed you, Madame. I can see now that you had nothing to do with the difficulties

I've been experiencing. Might I have a word with your niece? In private?"

"Wi-with Zee?" Serafina stammered. "In p-private?"

Zee could tell her aunt was gathering her courage to refuse. She was touched by Serafina's protective instincts, but right now those instincts were as unnecessary as they were unwelcome.

"Why, Monsieur, I...I hardly th-think that's necessary."

"It's all right, Auntie," Zee said quickly. "Why don't you go into the backroom and brew up one of your tisanes. I'm sure it will help calm your nerves."

Serafina gazed piteously at her. "Zee..."

"It's all right," she repeated, a little more firmly. "Really." She patted her aunt's arm and smiled reassuringly. It was more than all right, actually. A chance to be alone with her beloved Rene? That was cause for celebration! But even so, as her aunt, with a sad little nod and a reluctant backward glance, retreated from the room, Zee found a little of her confidence deserting her. Her gaze dropped once more. The rush of blood was so loud in her ears she could not even hear Rene's footsteps on the floorboards. Oh, but she felt his approach just the same. His powerful presence pervaded the atmosphere. She was paralyzed by it, enraptured, entranced.

"Zirondelle. Look at me."

Her name on his lips was the sweetest caress. His words were a command she could not disobey. She glanced up immediately, gaze locking with his piercing blue eyes. "Yes?"

"I know it's you."

"Wh-what? Me?" She drew in a shaky breath. "You do?" Well. It was only about time, wasn't it? After all, she'd known it was him for most of her life. He was her destiny, her fate, the other half of her soul.

"Yes. I know it's you who's cast this spell upon me."

Zee's heart sank. Was that all he was talking about? Disappointment fueled her defiance. She tossed her head and demanded, "And? What if it was?"

"Then you will remove it. At once."

"What if I won't?"

His eyes widened. "You would dare defy me?"

Would she? The thought shook her and, for just a moment, she considered backing down. She didn't want him angry with her, after all. Even if she weren't madly in love with the man, she still would never want to make an enemy of him—no one with any sense at all would want that! On the other hand, desperation was a powerful goad. At this point, she was willing to go pretty far to attract his attention. And if this was what it took, so be it.

Besides, foolish or not, she just could not bring herself to fear him all that much. She'd known him all her life. This was the same Rene Boudreaux who was so kind to her as a child, who'd comforted her as no one else could have following her parents' tragic and untimely deaths.

It was he who'd found her, hiding beneath a table in the funeral home, paging feverishly through a book of spells she'd taken from her grandmother's house, looking for something—anything—that might bring them back. Curses were not the only things with which vampires were familiar. They knew death and loss better than anyone else. When Rene had promised her she would not die from a broken heart, when he insisted no spell was necessary, that her parents had not really gone anywhere, that those we truly love will continue to live on eternally, enshrined in our hearts forever, Zee believed him.

Now, remembering that day, remembering all his

kindness—both then and after—a smile curved her lips. "Why not? I think I would. After all, I know you'd never hurt me." Not unless she wanted him to.

Rene sighed. "This is insupportable." He shook his head wearily and asked, "What is it you want from me, child?"

"Not very much." Other than for him to stop thinking of her as a child and recognize her finally as a woman, one who knew her own heart and was willing to be whatever he wanted or needed her to be. "Just one night. One night with you."

"What's that?" Rene stared at her in alarm. "No. Impossible. You don't know what you're asking for."

"I don't?" She smiled a little and teasingly said, "Well, if that's the case, it's all the more reason, isn't it?"

No matter what Rene might assume, Zee really didn't think it was possible that there was anything she didn't know about the man. Her family had always kept very meticulous records on the people they did business with—as a form of insurance, if nothing else—and Zee had studied those records in depth. She knew his history, his pain and his sorrow. She knew his tastes and predilections. She knew all about his illicit affair with her great-great-great-aunt Adeline.

The Doucettes were not long-lived in general, but Adeline had died even younger than was usual for one of their clan, consumed by her passion for Rene Boudreaux, or so the story went. Though most of the family seemed to regard Adeline's sad fate as a cautionary tale—a perfect example of why, especially when it came to matters of the heart, one should steer clear of vampires in general and Rene Boudreaux in particular—Zee had never found the story off-putting. Whatever had happened to Adeline, and Zee was not convinced anyone knew the full story there, she was sure it had not been Rene's fault. At least not entirely.

And even if it had been, so what? There were certainly worse ways to meet one's end.

It was possible Rene didn't know about the file of information her family had amassed about him, although Zee found it hard to imagine he could be so naïve that he didn't at least suspect they had one. Still, he couldn't believe her completely ignorant of his ways. He must have noticed the way she'd been dogging his footsteps these past months, yearning, learning, studying his every move. Why, she'd visited the sex club he owned and operated on Bourbon Street so frequently that she was now on a first-name basis with the bouncers and bartenders. She'd seen him in full Dom mode, dressed in black leather that fit him like a second skin and added further fuel to her fantasies. She'd watched while he demonstrated proper flogging techniques. She'd listened as he explained how best to discipline an unruly sub. She'd dreamed of one day experiencing all of that for herself.

In short, she'd done her homework. She knew exactly what she was risking, exactly what she was asking for as she repeated her request. "One night. With you. In your dungeon."

A shudder ran through his frame. It may have been nothing more than a sudden chill or a ghost walking over his grave, as the saying goes, but Zee didn't want to believe that was the case. She wanted to believe it was a sudden rush of heat that was affecting him. A desperate need to dominate her. An overwhelming desire to have her naked, bound and totally at his mercy.

Open, vulnerable, his—wasn't that exactly what she wanted too? Her heart soared with the sudden hope that tonight might see both their goals realized.

His stern gaze held hers for a moment longer. "And then you'll release me from your spell?"

Once again disappointment stabbed at her heart. Once again she ducked her head and sighed. "Then I will do whatever you ask of me."

"Very well." Rene's voice sounded unexpectedly grim. "If that's the way it has to be. Go and tell your aunt you're leaving. And be quick about it. I don't like to be kept waiting."

Zee nodded, not trusting herself to answer. Not trusting herself to say yes without adding Master. It was still too soon for that.

Out in the street, warm night air caressed Rene's skin and teased his tastebuds with a mélange of scents and flavors—bourbon, brown sugar, crawfish boil, dark coffee, rum—trivial things for which he had no longer any use. Ah, but there had been a time, he could still remember it, when he'd found them enjoyable, when such simple pleasures had the power to satisfy all his appetites. The sultry-sweet sound of a sax floated on the breeze and up ahead he could see a young couple dancing together on the banquette. They look happy, innocent, in love; for a moment, he envied them that. Once, he had been just like them—before time and loss had twisted his soul. The pleasures he craved now were darker, hotter, more intoxicating and far more dangerous. Like the pleasure of mastering Zirondelle Doucette.

To have her within his control, at his command, her body and mind—his to explore, to discover, to pleasure again and again. How he'd love to have the training of her. Oh, the things he could show her! He'd be the first to witness her response, the first to ever have her in any of a dozen different ways.

31

Such a thing was impossible, of course. He should put it from his mind. But he couldn't help thinking about it all the same. In fact, try as he might, these past few weeks that had been all he could think about. Given the way she'd been flitting about on the edges of his existence all that time, invading his thoughts, never leaving him a minute's peace, she deserved the flogging he had every intention of administering tonight. Why, she'd even haunted his dreams.

It had to be a spell. Had to be. And after all the money he'd given her family over the years! All the charms he'd purchased—all to ensure that just such a thing as this never occurred again. He should demand a refund. Not that it would do him any good.

He should have recognized right from the start what was happening to him. He should have confronted Zirondelle the first night she visited his club and ordered her then to keep her distance. Or, better yet, he should have simply left town years ago—back when he'd first realized that the uncommonly pretty child he'd grown so fond of, who he'd so enjoyed visiting and spending time with, was fast becoming an impossibly beautiful woman. One whose appeal he would never be able to resist.

He could still recall, even after nearly a decade, the shock he'd felt the day he'd first caught sight of that look in her eyes. Combining the innocent trust of a child with the needs of a woman and the devotion of a true submissive, it shook him to his soul. Even then, as inchoate as it was, it left him stunned, hungry, craving her with a desperation he had not felt in over a century.

It was wrong to feel the way he did about so young a girl, and he certainly had never acted on those feelings! But they tormented him all the same.

When one's desires can lead only to the

destruction of precisely that which one holds most dear, it's best to distance oneself. Or, better yet, not to love at all. So he'd told himself, over and over again. And so he'd kept his distance, fearing for Zirondelle's wellbeing, hoping in time his own madness would pass. And mostly succeeding, until her innocent spell had ensnared him. Until her childish capriciousness had caused her to stray into dangerous territory, landing them both in bigger trouble than she knew.

Now, as she joined him on the banquette, looking far too happy, excited and pleased with herself, looking like everything he wanted—and everything he knew he shouldn't allow himself to have—he wondered how it had come to this. Perhaps he'd been fooling himself all along. Perhaps all his experience had taught him nothing. Perhaps it was his fate to always repeat the same mistakes. For her sake, he hoped to God that was not the case.

All the same, as he placed a hand on her back to guide her over to where his car was parked, he couldn't help wondering if he wasn't just leading them both down the path of irresistible temptation.

It's Voodoo. It has to be. That's the only acceptable explanation.

A spell, after all, could be lifted. A curse could be removed. Their effects would dissipate like the evening mist and all would be as it had been before. Anything else was simply too hopeless to contemplate.

Rene unlocked his car. "Get in," he said as he held the passenger door open.

Zirondelle glanced at the car in surprise. "We're driving? Why? Where are we going?"

It seemed an odd time for her to start raising objections—not that she shouldn't object to what he had planned for her. Not that he shouldn't be happy that she'd finally come to her senses. And he was happy. Perfectly so. "Where do you think we're going? I'm taking you back to my house. Isn't that what you wanted?"

"Oh." Her tongue emerged to nervously lick at her plush, pink lips. She gazed at him uncertainly. "Yes. I-I guess."

Rene tried hard not to think about how soft and delicious those luscious lips would feel pressed against his own, how easily they'd part for his tongue, how urgently he longed to taste them. He raised an eyebrow. "Have you changed your mind? It's not too late for that, you know. Release me now and promise never to do such a thing again and we'll both forget it ever happened."

Immediately, Zirondelle's chin rose. "No," she said quickly. "Who said anything about changing my mind? We have a deal. Let's go." Suiting her actions to her words, she slipped quickly into the seat. She pulled the door shut and stared defiantly at him through the window.

Rene sighed wearily. As he rounded the front of the car, he tried hard to ignore the treacherous feeling of relief that was filling his heart. There was nothing to feel relieved about. Nothing at all.

The low-slung sports car was sleek and elegant and somewhat understated, much like the man to whom it belonged, Zee couldn't help but reflect. But that was only on the outside. Beneath the unassuming surfaces, the gleaming midnight blue paint and butter-soft, oyster-gray leather, the genteel manners and studied calm, they both thrummed with power.

He's taking me home! Her heart beat faster at the thought of their tryst taking place in such an intimate setting. It was all she could do to keep from grinning like an idiot. She hadn't dreamed she would be this lucky—especially not tonight! All the same, she couldn't help feeling just a little intimidated, too. So much for being up-to-date on her information. She'd been assuming they would go to his club. She had no idea he even had a dungeon in his house. Not even in Adeline's diary had there been any mention of such a thing.

She was still fairly certain he lived alone, however. So, unlike at the club, there would be no witnesses to what went on tonight. If things went bad, if they took a turn for the ugly, there'd be no one to hear her scream, no one at all to intervene.

"So, why the sudden interest?" Rene broke the silence to ask.

"Who said it's sudden?" Zee replied, eyeing him cautiously. It was true they'd seen far too little of each other in the past ten years, but did he really not know how she long she'd yearned for him?

"Oh?" Rene's jaw clenched. His hands tightened on the steering wheel. "What are you saying then? You've experimented with such activities before? When? Where? With who?"

"What?" Zee frowned. "Wait. Are you talking about...BDSM?"

"Yes, of course. For want of a better term," Rene replied. "It's not one I favor. What else did you think we were talking about?"

"Oh, I don't know." Zee quickly brushed the question aside. "Nothing. It's not important." She'd thought they were talking about him, about them, about the heart and source of her real interest. But that, she supposed, was simply too much to hope for. "No, I haven't experimented very much at all." There was no one else she wanted to do this with, no one else she trusted. No one else she wished to surrender to.

"Then why have you been pushing so hard? Is it all just idle curiosity? Why choose me?"

Ah, there was a question. Zee felt her lips curve into a small smile. If only she knew the answer to it. But who could ever say why they'd fallen in love? Love wasn't math or science, something you could quantify or dissect. Love was a mystery. It was magical, mystical and very much like the Voodoo spell he claimed to be under. "It's not just curiosity. I told you: I've been interested for a while. And why not you? Why not the best?"

"Hmph." Was that a pleased smile teasing the corners of Rene's lips? Zee wasn't sure, but she thought it might be. "Well," he replied at last, grudgingly. "I certainly can't fault your logic there."

It was a short drive to the Garden District where Rene's home was located. The house was well maintained, but Zee would not have been at all surprised to learn that the early 19th century mansion looked just the same now as it had when it was first constructed. Only the mature landscaping surrounding the structure gave witness to the march of time.

The room he eventually ushered her into was located at the back of the house and here, finally, was something different! Given its location, the room had probably originally been meant to function as a morning room. A vampire would have no earthly use for such things, of course, so why not turn it into something vastly more entertaining, like a dungeon? She chided herself for having imagined something subterranean. This was New Orleans after all, where even burials took place above ground.

As she glanced around, taking in her surroundings, Zee couldn't suppress a tiny shiver of hunger, of longing...and yes, okay, perhaps a little bit of fear. The room was dark, its windows draped and shuttered, its walls painted a deep burgundy over oak wainscoting. It was intimate without being claustrophobic, warm and...welcoming somehow. She supposed that was due to the furnishings. Mostly well-oiled leather and wood, there was something substantial and vaguely comforting about them. They gave one the impression of having aged and mellowed with time. Of being solid and trustworthy. Only the shiny steel clamps and restraints, gleaming dully in the dim light, struck a modern and somewhat sinister note.

Rene escorted her to a small, curtained changing area and left her there with the demand she strip and await his return. She shed her clothes slowly, hampered in part by the surprising shakiness of her fingers.

"Are you sure this is what you want, Zee?" her aunt had asked when Zee had told her where she was going.

She'd nodded and smiled, feeling the same sense of certainty she was feeling now. "Yes, Auntie. I've never been more sure about anything."

All her life it had been Rene. Even as a young girl she'd dreamed of him. Every fantasy she'd ever had had centered around him. She'd had boyfriends, of course, one or two of whom she'd even imagined herself in love with. But no one had ever come close to touching that place in her heart that belonged only to Rene. Eventually she'd been forced to the realization that no one ever would.

As she grew older, her dreams had changed, but not very much. What mostly changed was that now she had a name for her desires; she had a context for her feelings. She knew exactly what she wanted. She wanted to submit to him. To surrender her heart to his care. To place her body in his capable hands. To hold nothing back and give him everything he demanded. And if it happened that those demands included a touch of pain, so much the better. That was something else she'd learned about herself, how the pain transmuted into pleasure, how it made love better, sweeter, hotter. How she longed for it.

Just a touch of pain, however. A hint—no more. Unrelieved suffering, either mental or physical, was no one's desire. She was equally certain of that.

Zee had read the letters Rene had written to Adeline. She'd wept at his pain when he'd begged his lover to let him change her in a last-ditch effort to save her life after she'd fallen so gravely ill. She'd wept even harder at the letter written after Adeline had refused him, after she'd chosen death for herself and doomed Rene to centuries of tormented loneliness. That sort of pain was not something she would have wished on anyone, let alone someone as dear to her as Rene.

If it had been Zee in Adeline's place, their story would have had a far different ending. She would have sacrificed anything to be with him. So what if the life of a vampire was dark and unnatural, as Adeline had claimed? It was the only life he had to offer his lover. How could she reject it out of hand? How could she choose to abandon him to his lonely fate, when she might have shared it with him?

Still, Zee couldn't help but be grateful for Adeline's decision. After all, it had opened a door for her. It had given Zee the chance to aspire to something even better than she would have had otherwise. Maybe she couldn't unbreak Rene's heart, but she could still hope to be the woman who brought that organ back to life, who healed his heart—just as once he'd healed hers.

The hiss of the curtains being whisked brusquely aside was the only warning she had. She turned and promptly lost her breath. There he was. Standing right in front of her. The look on his face and in his eyes was one she'd never seen there before, stern and autocratic, even more intense than when he'd been at his club. He was wearing leather pants, so thin and soft they molded to his thighs, and a leather vest that left his arms and most of his chest bare. Those she'd seen before, of course, but never like this, never close enough to touch. Now more than ever, the sight left her weak in the knees. Perhaps it was knowing that he wore them for her, but once again she felt the compulsion to fall at his feet. This time, she gave into it—or she would have, if he hadn't stopped her.

"No." Even as she started to lower herself, he grabbed her by the arm, keeping her erect. There was an unrestrained hoarseness to his voice when he spoke. "Not yet. Not here. Go stand over there. In the light."

She nodded her head once, feeling lighter than air and powerful beyond belief. The hand with which he held her arm vibrated, as though he could barely maintain his control. The knowledge she could affect him to this extent thrilled her. When he released her, she walked proudly over to the place he'd indicated, beneath the ornate brass and crystal ceiling fixture and stood there waiting.

The sway of Zirondelle's hips riveted Rene's attention as he slowly followed her across the room. He circled her deliberately, struggling for control while instinct urged him to fall upon her naked form and feast at her throat. She reminded him so much of Adeline. Why had he never realized that before? Why was she choosing to taunt him in this manner? Perhaps someone else had bespelled them both? If that was so, it was cruel beyond belief.

He'd loved Adeline with all his heart. Despite what her family had believed, he would have willingly sold his soul to save her. He'd have given anything to keep her from harm. In the end, however, he had nothing of any value to offer her. At least, nothing she was willing to accept. Why was that? Why had she rebuffed his offer? He'd spent years, decades, asking himself those same questions, never finding any answers. Was it somehow his fault? Had he frightened her that much? Had she spied the darkness within him and chosen death instead? Maybe he had held on too tightly. Maybe she had been just that desperate to escape from him.

If he fell now for Zirondelle, would the same thing happen again? Could he save either one of them? Or was it already too late to prevent another disaster?

"I don't know why you insisted on coming here tonight," he growled, still struggling for control. "And I still think this is a mistake. But, so be it. From here on in, you're mine. Mine to do with as I see fit. You will do as I say. You will take what you're given. And I hope for your sake you realize what you've let yourself in for."

"I do," she said, boldly raising her eyes to meet his gaze.

"Silence!" Rene barked in response. "Did I say you could speak? I thought you said you were familiar with how this works. You are to say nothing unless you are asked a direct question. And then you will answer only 'yes, Master' or 'thank you, Master,' as the situation dictates. And that is all you will say. Is that understood?"

Zirondelle released a shaky sigh. A tremulous smile curved her lips as she answered, "Yes, Master."

Rene ground his teeth. It was obscene the way her voice caressed the words and she looked altogether too happy for someone who he'd just had to reprimand, entirely too pleased with herself. Where was the fear? Where was the remorse? Where was the submission?

"Why are you doing this?" he snapped. "You're obviously not serious about any of it. Is it all a game to you? Casting spells, playing childish pranks—have you no idea how much danger you've placed us both in with your foolishness?"

The smile slid away from Zirondelle's face. She gazed at him darkly, silently. Her eyes grew hooded, speculative, remote.

Rene's temper continued to disintegrate. "Answer me, damn it!" he ordered, abandoning the very protocol he'd just laid out for her. "Tell me what you're up to."

"It's not a game. And I'm not a child any longer. And I never cast any stupid spell. So if you're really expecting me to release you when we're done here, you're out of luck. I'm doing this because I love you. How can you not know that?"

"No." Rene took a step back, recoiling from her words as he would from sunlight—both had the power to destroy him. "Stop it. Don't say things you don't mean."

"But I do mean it," Zirondelle insisted. "I've always loved you, for as long as I can remember. Tonight, I saw a chance to spend some time with you, to show you how I feel, to force you to notice me, so I took it."

"So it's an act? Is that what you're saying? All your supposed interest is nothing more than a ploy to garner my attention?" Rene fought a sudden urge to shake her 'til her teeth rattled. "Is that why you've never tried any of this before?" Why was he so surprised? She certainly wasn't the first woman who'd pretended to share his interests—only to realize too late all that it entailed. Only to recant her words, her promises after he'd given her his heart.

Zirondelle shook her head. "Of course not. That would be stupid. Who would do something like that? It's what I crave too. But…only with you. You're what I want. You're all I want. And this is part of what you are."

"Silence," Rene growled. Hope and fear warred within him and he couldn't listen to any more of this. It was time to test her resolve, to challenge her brave words. It was time to see for himself just what it was she wanted.

Zee watched as Rene stalked over to the large cabinet that she'd assumed housed his toys. He opened the door, grabbed something from the shelf and strode back to where she stood waiting. Her eyes widened at the sight of the ball-gag clenched in his fist. Why bother explaining what she was and wasn't to say if she wasn't to be allowed to say anything at all?

"Open," Rene ordered.

Zee opened her mouth reluctantly and allowed him to fit the gag snugly into place. Her head swam. The rubber tasted bitter but she could not deny the small thrill that shot through her as it filled her mouth. Her nipples tightened. Her pussy pulsed with need. Who knew such a small thing could turn her on so quickly?

Still, as Rene took her arm and led her over to the large cross that dominated one whole corner of the room, she couldn't help but worry. Her heart pounded fiercely. They hadn't even discussed safewords—not that words would do her any good at the moment, of course. But shouldn't they at least have established some sort of signal? Wasn't that a basic requirement? Safe. Sane. Consensual. She recited the words in her head, wondering how many of them actually applied to her current situation. Did any of them?

If his plan was to test her trust in him, he was doing a fabulous job!

Her nerves spiked higher after he'd fastened her in

place and left her. She slowed her breathing as best she could and tried hard not to hyperventilate. Passing out before they'd even gotten started was no way to prove her sincerity. His footsteps receded across the room and she could only wait and wonder what implement of destruction he was planning to use on her. She didn't have long to wait. All those trips to his club had not been for nothing. She recognized the swishing sounds she heard behind her. So. He'd gone for the flogger. She supposed it could be worse.

As the first stroke landed across her upper back, however, she realized she'd seriously misjudged him. It wasn't just better than worse, it was...perfect. A quick splash of heat. A slow, spreading burn. Lightning fast strikes that brought tears to her eyes, that stung her flesh as though she'd sat too close to the fire on a cold winter's night.

The constant barrage locked down her thoughts, leaving her mind wide open to sensation. And then, just when she feared it might all become too much...it stopped.

Rene pressed against her from behind and Zee moaned weakly. Her head was spinning and everywhere his body made contact with hers, her skin sizzled. She was surprised to realize she was trembling on the brink of orgasm.

"Well?" he asked, his lips close to her ear. "Is this what you want?"

And just like that, Zee tumbled over the edge. She moaned and nodded, sagging against him as the tremors seized her. Yes. Oh, yes. Oh, God, yes. This was definitely what she'd wanted. How could he doubt it?

Rene was breathing heavily as he released her—first her ankles and then her wrists—keeping one hand anchored at her waist to steady her. Carefully, he turned her to face him. She leaned against him, still shaky, still not quite trusting her legs to hold her up. He tenderly removed the ball-gag from her mouth and stared down at her, his eyes dark as he studied her face.

"Just so you know," he said at last, "I've always loved you as well."

Then, before Zee had even an instant to process his words, he kissed her. Gasping slightly in surprise, she wound her arms around his neck and held on tight. As he claimed her mouth, she did the same to his, pressing herself against him, delighting in the feel of his strong hands caressing her skin, soothing away the heat.

When he finally let her go she glanced up at him. "You can't blame this on the Voodoo, you know," she told him, needing to get that straight. "There was no spell. No curse. No nothing. Not on my end. If you're really in love with me, that's all on you. You did that to yourself."

"Silence." Heat raced across her skin once again as his hand made contact with her ass. She squeaked in surprise. "Did I give you permission to speak?"

Zee bit her lip. She held his gaze an instant longer, then lowered her eyes and softly whispered, "No, Master."

Rene sighed. Gently, he brushed her hair back behind her ears. "We'll talk about that later."

Zee couldn't be sure, but she thought she heard the hint of a chuckle in his voice.

"In the meantime, I can see I have my work cut out for me. There's still so much you have to learn, so much I'll have to teach you. Why, I'll probably have to spend years training you, an entire lifetime in all likelihood. Won't I?"

His voice trembled just a little on those last two words. The doubt and the longing and the slight uncertainty in his tone filled Zee's heart with warmth. Try as she might, she couldn't keep from smiling as she met his gaze once more and happily answered, "Yes, Master."

Bourbon Street Blues *by Skylar Kade*

Drinking a hurricane on Bourbon Street her first night in New Orleans made absolutely no sense, which was exactly why Alexa Huston did it. It was a Wednesday night, but enough tourists and local college kids lined the street to give her an idea of just how overwhelming—and scandalous—her new neighborhood would probably be on the weekends. Though her new apartment was a few streets away, she was still in the French Quarter, or, as her mother had taken to calling it, "Sin by the Mississippi."

Looking at the Hustler store and the myriad strip joints, she hated to admit that her mother wasn't all too wrong. Still, whether it was the long day flying from Wyoming to Louis Armstrong Airport or the half-serving of alcohol she'd already imbibed, Bourbon Street actually seemed kind of charming. It was certainly not a sensible place for her to be, which only increased its appeal.

While she scanned the street, taking in the tourists throwing beads from second-story balconies and the young men high-fiving each other as they exited strip clubs, her stomach rumbled in a not-so-subtle reminder that she hadn't eaten in a while.

On the corner, the words Bourbon House glowed from a sign, beckoning her in to eat. It seemed as good a place as any, if a little upscale, but Alexa figured after her hellish day, she deserved a little luxury for dinner. After all, who knew when her suitcases would miraculously show up at the airport? She could be stuck in these clothes for days until the moving van arrived. She needed to enjoy herself while she was still presentable. The last sips of her hurricane bubbled through the straw and she chucked the empty souvenir cup into her tote before heading for the corner.

She entered the nearly empty restaurant and claimed a seat at the bar. A quick scan of the menu revealed all the delicious native dishes she'd discovered in her thorough research of the town. The bartender sauntered over, an open smile on her young face. "What can I get you?"

Alexa rubbed her hands together in glee. "I'll start with the alligator boudin, then have a bowl of the seafood gumbo, and a half dozen oysters Bienville."

The bartender arched her eyebrow. "Hungry?"

A huge grin broke across her face. "Starving. And it's my first night in New Orleans, so I feel a distinct urge to try everything."

The woman leaned on the bar. "Then you must have a Sazerac with your meal. It's a local drink with bourbon, absinthe, and bitters. I definitely think you can handle it."

"Done!" Alexa could feel her hurricane buzz lapping away the tension in her shoulders. A drink with dinner sounded like a perfectly good idea.

While she waited for her meal, she whipped out her smartphone and delved back into her favorite gothic romance. She couldn't get enough of Wuthering Heights, and she imagined such a turbulent romance would be right at home in her new city. New Orleans had that tragic, romantic vibe down perfectly. While Alexa had no interest in a high-drama romance—no, she was more the love at first sight type—she still got shivers every time Heathcliff touched Catherine.

Time slipped away as she read, only snapping back into place when the waitress placed a glass of water and platter of boudin in front of her. She wasn't usually an experimental eater, but Alexa had done enough research before moving there to know she needed to try alligator at least once. It was one of a long list of things to do that she'd written before flying across the country.

She'd already crossed off her number one item: get out of the state, despite the disapproval of her parents. Twenty-seven years in the same town was quite long enough, thank you very much. And after that spectacular break up with her ex, her small hometown had become even more stifling.

Besides, she couldn't very well pass up the only tenure-track teaching position she'd been offered. Openings for English professors were few and far between, and the local University of Wyoming campus could only keep her on part time. Secretly, she knew her parents had appreciated that she couldn't really leave home, but she'd been in remission for so long that the foundation of their fears had crumbled.

Geronimo, she thought before biting into a ball of alligator, rice, and aromatic spices. The flavor burst across her tongue, so far from the traditional American fare she'd grown up on that she knew it would quickly become an addiction. She moaned and closed her eyes, taking another fearless bite.

"I've never seen someone enjoy boudin so much." The deep, syrupy voice slid down her spine.

She swallowed and opened her eyes to find the bar stool next to her occupied by a gorgeous man. His dark brown skin matched his decadent voice, and the leather jacket encasing his broad shoulders did unspeakable things for his body. The overhead lighting glinted off his shaved head while his laughing golden eyes captured and held her attention.

Back home, she'd eschewed bars, hating the whole scene and feeling sleazy every time a guy talked to her. Not that she'd been in years, but she remembered the skin-crawling effect of a drunken man trying to flirt. And though this man had invaded her personal bubble about five inches back, she didn't want him to leave.

"My first taste of New Orleans," she finally answered.

He slapped his hand against his chest. "Non! Oh, cher, what a delight you are."

Without thinking, she nudged her plate towards him. "Join me?" She'd never been so forward, but something about this man lowered all her defenses. His wide grin warmed her chest like the Sazerac she sipped, but with a headier kick at the end.

He popped a boudin ball into his mouth and gave her a lusty wink. "Delicious. I'm Baron."

"Alexa." She held out her hand and instead of shaking it, he lifted it to his lips and presssed a kiss to her palm. Southern hospitality indeed.

The liberty didn't faze her, though it should have. But his face was honest and familiar; she didn't take back her hand until he let her go.

Her gumbo arrived, breaking the tension—thankfully. Without skipping a beat, Baron poked into her day, laughing as she regaled him with her disastrous travel story which, in hindsight, was too ridiculous not to be hilarious.

Somehow, through her soup and their shared oysters, she spilled her moving-cross-country story in spite of her normal reticence. Whether the alcohol or the man loosened her tongue, she'd never know, but she couldn't seem to stop herself.

"Let me buy you dessert, cher, then I'll show you around the French Quarter."

She should have turned him down, but how long had it been since she'd had a relaxing night out? Since a gorgeous man had flirted with her, but been a perfect gentleman? Her unfailing instincts screamed his trustworthiness. She swept her hands across her jeans, feeling the reassuring press of her pocket knife, then threw caution to the wind. "Only if the dessert is chocolate."

He threw back his head and laughed. "You drive a hard bargain, Miss Alexa, but I know the Bourbon House has just what you need." He beckoned for the bartender and whispered into her ear. "Merci."

"Have you lived here your whole life?" She wanted to know more about this man.

"Indeed. New Orleans is in my blood. I couldn't imagine living anywhere else."

"That must be nice," she sighed. "Though if my day so far is any indication, this city is going to set its hooks in me and my poor mother will never get me to come home."

"She will have to visit you here, and see what a wonderful life you're building for yourself."

Alexa blushed at the compliment, premature though it was. "Oh hush."

By the time dessert arrived, she would have sworn she'd known Baron her whole life. The only time she'd forged such an immediate connection was with her childhood friend Sara. Long-ago pain stabbed at Alexa. Sara had never made it out of the children's cancer ward of their local St. Jude's hospital.

"Eat, Alexa." Baron offered her a forkful of something that looked delicious and smelled divine. "It's not magic, but it's so soothing you'd swear the pastry chef was a Voodoo priestess."

Her lips quirked in a smile and she took the fork. True to his word, the cake melted in her mouth in a sweet, salty, chocolate explosion. "What is this?"

Baron took a bite and washed it down with a sip of his bourbon. "Chocolate pecan crunch cake. My very favorite."

They didn't talk until the plate was clean—yes, it was that good. After, when the bartender had cleared their plate, she reached for her wallet, willing to pay whatever exorbitant amount they wanted for that incredible meal.

Baron set his hand on hers. "I don't think so, cher. Dinner is on me." Before she could protest, he handed a stack of bills to the bartender with a wink, then turned Alexa on her stool so she faced him. "You can pay me back by letting me see the wonder on your face as you see New Orleans for the first time. Come along!"

He tucked her hand into the crook of his arm, then led her from the restaurant like a perfect gentleman. Yes, he opened the door for her, and stood sentinel over her as the wandered down the middle of Bourbon Street, but not once did Baron make her feel like a fragile invalid. She'd escaped more than just the cold winter by leaving Wyoming.

A block down the street, jazz music filtered through a wrought-iron archway. Alexa tugged Baron in that direction, seeing a quartet of musicians through a crowd of people. They entered the courtyard and Baron guided her around the edges of the throng until they broke into the makeshift dance floor. A handful of couples swayed under the moonlight, the heady scent of magnolias perfuming the air.

With a graceful flourish, Baron swept her into his arms, one strong hand settling on her lower back. He twined their fingers together and brought her tight against his chest. Her breath stuttered at his closeness and the

51

heat radiating off his body. The intimacy of the moment, perfectly innocent yet seductive, raced through her blood. It was Catherine and Heathcliff on the moors, Elizabeth and Mr. Darcy in the ballroom, Alice and her Mad Hatter down the rabbit hole.

One song stretched into two, then four, until Alexa was convinced they could dance there until sunlight streamed across the sky. With each tune she pressed herself closer against her mystery man. He smelled like New Orleans, sweet and peppery and biting. His cheek rested against her head and Alexa closed her eyes, imagining a whirlwind southern romance.

"I am not the one for you, pretty girl." His voice rumbled up through his chest, imprinting every word onto her body. "But my city is nothing if not a true romantic." She tilted up to see the truth in his eyes, disappointing and eminently reassuring. He leaned down to lay a chaste, searing kiss on her lips. "That is not to say that I would not enjoy you for a night." Baron waggled his eyebrows and she couldn't help but laugh, as if she'd done the same thing a million times with him. Why did he seem so familiar?

His scent clung to her as he danced them to the edges of the crowd then led her back to the street. Drunk on the music, on him, Alexa melted against his side when he slung an arm around her shoulder. Baron talked about Bourbon Street, pointing out Pat O'Brien's bar, the Royal Sonesta Hotel, the Old Absinthe House, and the Marie Laveau House of Voodoo.

"Maybe I should get myself a love charm."

Baron snugged her tighter against his side. "No need, cher, when you've got me." He laughed, but if it was a joke, she didn't get it. "I bet you've never had a beignet, hmm? Probably endless boring doughnuts in that hospital ward, but no beignets."

She nodded. When had she told him about her cancer treatments? A flash of memory hit her, then vanished, only leaving her with the odd, ancient impression of Baron's face floating above her in the ICU, giving her that cheeky smile.

Alexa shook it off. "Maybe that Sazerac wasn't a great idea. Beignets, however, sound like an excellent cure."

Baron turned right down St. Ann, taking them through darkened streets and past alleys that would have been haunting, had she been with anyone else. But with Baron, she felt safe. Her uncanny instincts at work again.

His stream of conversation never ceased as he told her about Hurricane Katrina and watching his city pull itself up and rebuild. Conversation turned back to her, and once again she found herself babbling on about her itch to move away from home and how fortunate she was to have been chosen as Tulane's newest English professor.

"They are lucky to have you." Baron slipped a few dollars into the hat of a man singing Amazing Grace on the corner, tipping an imaginary hat in his direction. The man did a double-take, crossed himself, and continued his song. Alexa could feel the man's eyes boring into their backs.

Odd.

She could just make out the sign for the Café du Monde, another item on her New Orleans to-do list. This was turning out to be quite the productive night, all thanks to Baron. With the promise of beignets and café au lait, she didn't give the minstrel another thought.

The café was packed, but somehow Baron found them a table in the corner where she could watch the crowds. He ordered, then tucked a few folded bills under the napkin holder on the table.

Within minutes, their food arrived. "Be careful of all that powdered sugar, cher. You give a man ideas when it be sweetening your skin." Beignet halfway to her mouth, Alexa blushed. She carefully nibbled at the edge, watching the soft powder drift down to the wire café table. Baron sipped his coffee and eyed her over the rim. "Maybe that's just what you need, girl."

She snorted, the mound of sugar that topped her beignet puffing out like a sweet cloud of smoke. "Yeah, because my last relationship was such a joyride."

With a tut tut, Baron shook his head and stuffed a whole beignet into his mouth. His tongue flicked out to sensually lick at the sugar on his lips. "He was not meant for you. Besides," he looked her up and down, "you held yourself back."

Indignant, she slammed her coffee down on the table. It sloshed over the edges and spilled onto her hand. "I did not! He is the one who cheated on me, after promising to move here with me." All the fight seeped from her body. "He'd been cheating on me a long time, though."

"I know."

She looked up at his knowing eyes through the wisps of her newly cut bangs. "How?"

"I been watching you, cher."

Like a rubber band snapping into place, she knew her earlier memory had been right. "When I was a child? In the hospital? But how?"

Baron shook his head, a rueful smile curling around the edges of another beignet. "Secrets, secrets. But New Orleans is full of all kinds of magic, old and new. This place be good for you, if you let it."

Before she could even start to unravel the madness

Baron unleashed—and she knew he wasn't lying, she could feel it in the pit of her stomach, as true as anything she'd ever known—he snagged his money and tipped her a nod.

She watched him walk to the counter pay, then she flicked her attention away. A few tables away, a young couple kissed powdered sugar off each other's lips; another small group of women laughed riotously; the man next to her scribbled in a worn journal, his long fingers curled around his fountain pen. He had a poet's hair, tumbling off his scalp to brush against his broad shoulders. While his hair might be all sweet words and romance, the sinful quirk to his wide mouth told a different story. His lips curled into a full-blown grin that hit her like a whack to the stomach.

That one.

When she looked back, Baron was gone. She darted her head around, but found no sign of him.

A busboy darted over, clearing his empty coffee cup and the beignet tray now filled only with powdered sugar.

"Ma'am, is this yours?" He held up a leather bracelet with an etched metal shield on it.

She opened her mouth to say no, until she heard a deep whisper. Take it, cher. Looking over her shoulder, she saw nothing. No Baron, no one.

Curious, she held out her hand for it, and the busboy dropped it into her palm as if it had burned him. She studied the symbol imprinted on the silver, a cross on what looked like a three-tiered pyramid.

The symbol was familiar. She couldn't place it at first, but then her research came back in a rush. Papa Ghede, one of the Loa. The Voodoo gods.

Clever girl. This time when she looked around for the voice, she caught the eye of the man next to her. Her heart galloped like the New Orleans carriage horses at full speed.

His green eyes seared into her, as if they could see to the depths of her soul. Where Baron's gaze had been warm and comforting, this man was all fire and passion.

She didn't breathe until his attention flickered to the bracelet, then back to her. "Baron Samedi, huh? Lucky girl. He's pretty stingy with his attentions."

"Excuse me?" The world was still tilting under her feet, and his mellow, whiskey voice wasn't helping any. How was a woman expected to focus when she was melting into a pool of desire?

He rose from his chair, his athletic form towering over her, before he knelt by her side and ran his thumb along the bracelet. One lock of black hair dipped across his face in stark contrast to those bright eyes. When his hand bumped against hers, she gasped at the bite of electricity.

He grinned again. Hot damn. She was staring, which she knew had to be rude, but nothing could tear her away until she drank her fill of his face. He swallowed twice, and she wanted to trace the column of his throat with her tongue.

"What were you saying about Baron?" she squeaked out.

Shaking his head, he gathered himself then answered. "He's one of the loa. That's his symbol."

"Papa Ghede?"

"One and the same."

Chills zipped down her spine, the pieces falling into place in her mind. Impossible.

She smiled. Certainly not sensible.

When the man grinned back at her, she couldn't help reaching out to rest her hand atop his on the table. "I'm Alexa. Want to join me?"

He lifted her hand to his lips, kissing her exactly where Baron had. This time, though, that warm tingling turned into something altogether alive and fluttering in her stomach. "I'm Stephan, and it would be my pleasure."

He grabbed his pen and journal, threw them into a leather laptop bag, then scooted Baron's unoccupied seat closer to her. She flagged down the waiter and ordered another coffee, hoping this would be one long night.

As Stephan's body heat warmed her side, she took in the café once more, wanting to imprint this moment on her brain. The crowds hadn't changed. The Mississippi still flowed behind them. The French Quarter still bustled with evening revelers.

But her world had tipped upside down, and it was down the Loa hole for her, just like a Cajun Alice. Four black horses trotted down the street, their driver peeking around the side of his carriage to give her a lusty wink and a wave.

Baron. Papa Ghede. She didn't know when she'd see him again, but he'd been right about one thing—New Orleans was a true romantic.

Ghost of a Chance *by Sydney Somers*

It didn't look like a haunted house.

Holly Clarke stared at the three-story house between swipes of the wiper blades across the windshield of her rental car.

Less than five minutes after her plane touched down in Louisiana, the heavy gray skies had erupted in torrential downpours. Although it had taken over an hour to find Beau Arbor House—nearly three times longer than her GPS had originally promised—she was still drenched from her mad dash to pick up her rental.

"Turn left in .2 miles."

Tempted to toss the useless GPS out the window, Holly settled for silencing it with a stab of her finger. She would have ended up in a bayou had she taken the next *left*.

Following a car-shaking boom of thunder, she turned off the vehicle and threw open the door. Her earlier discomfort at being back in New Orleans, the last stop on her story assignment, had nearly faded. Driving the dark, rainy streets hadn't brought back nearly as many memories of Sam as she'd feared when her editor added the Most Haunted City in America to her assignment itinerary.

Beau Arbor House had merited barely half a dozen hits by the almighty Google when Holly had researched the place two days ago. With dozens of haunted houses catering to Big Easy tourists, she couldn't imagine why this one warranted a mention in her article.

Arguing that point with her editor and best friend, Lena, would be pointless. Holly could be done with her assignment and on a plane bound for home before she'd ever sway Lena, once the woman's mind was made up. She trusted her friend's judgment, though, except when it came to Holly's love life. The last time she took Lena's advice on that front she'd ended up with a broken heart.

Grabbing her bags from the passenger seat, Holly bolted from the car, slamming the door behind her. It took only seconds to sprint past moss-covered trees and up the curved stone staircase to the covered front porch, but the rain still managed to soak her all over again.

Shivering, she set her bags down and wiped the rain from her face.

In front of her, the door swung inward with a heart-jarring creak.

Stumbling back a step on instinct, Holly then swore under her breath at the overreaction, blaming the goose bumps that raced across her skin on her wet clothes. Beau Arbor wasn't any more haunted than the five other bed and breakfasts she'd visited already. The food and eccentric staff had proven far spookier than any of the sightings and unexplained sounds the other B&Bs were supposedly famous for.

She was batting 0 for 5 in the haunting department and even accounting for dark, rainy nights and hinges in need of oiling, she didn't see that changing any time soon.

"Ms. Clarke?" A soft Cajun accent preceded the middle-aged woman who appeared in the doorway. Barely taller than Holly's shoulder, the woman cocked her head, her otherwise flawless caramel face undermined by an unexpected scowl.

Holly opened her mouth.

"I'm Charlotte," the woman interrupted, her intimidating gaze openly sizing Holly up.

Caught off guard by the scrutiny, she shifted in place. "Sorry for the late arrival—"

"You best hurry inside. I don't have much time. It's nearly nine o'clock." The woman spun away from the door, her long pleated skirt twirling up in a black wave of fabric tamed only by the thick braid falling down the middle of her back.

Dressing for the part? That was new.

"I'm in mourning," Charlotte clarified, though Holly hadn't said a word aloud.

Left to close the door, Holly finally grabbed her bags and stepped inside. Another shiver crawled up her spine at the thought of Charlotte seeming to read her mind. She shrugged it off, along with the sensation that she might be better off putting her fate in the hands of a malfunctioning GPS.

Charlotte was already halfway up an ornate mahogany staircase to the left of the main parlor and showed no sign of checking to see if Holly followed. Darting a quick glance overhead at the impressive stained-glass chandelier hanging overhead, she trailed after the housekeeper who definitely scored points on the creepiness scale.

If nothing else, Holly would be picking her next assignment for Lena's travel website, and sun, sand, and tropical drinks were at the top of her list. She'd heard enough ghost stories in the last couple of weeks to last a phantom's lifetime. Strangely enough, Charlotte seemed to be in too much of a hurry to fill her in on Beau Arbor's history.

Every other B&B owner had barely given her time to turn the car off before they were filling her in on each place's haunting details. While Holly knew Beau Arbor House was supposedly haunted by two brothers who'd both loved and lost the same woman near the end of the Civil War, she'd anticipated a more detailed recounting when she'd arrived.

From somewhere below the music of a fiddle drifted up, and Holly looked over the rail in search of the source.

"Ms. Clarke?" All but tapping her toes, Charlotte waited at the top of the second floor.

She hurried to join her. "What happens at nine?"

"I leave." With another head-to-toe survey that barely masked her skepticism, Charlotte carried on down the hall.

Wondering what she'd done to annoy the other woman, Holly followed. "I'm sorry if waiting for me made you late for something. My GPS—"

"The spirits don't care about your GPS."

"Spirits," Holly echoed. The Beau Arbor staff may have skipped the history lesson, but certainly didn't waste any time playing up the ghost angle.

The fiddle music grew louder, and Holly glanced over her shoulder, hoping to catch a peek at the person playing. "They won't be playing all night, will they?"

The woman arched a brow. "Depends on William's mood." She checked her watch and pulled a key from a pocket in her skirt before opening the door. "Oscar is the louder one."

"Another guest," Holly guessed.

"Hardly. Though our resident vampire is the one most likely to keep you awake."

"Hope he's not hungry." If Charlotte was pulling out all the stops, Holly didn't mind playing along.

Charlotte didn't appreciate the humor. She didn't even crack a smile.

"I was being metaphorical," the housekeeper continued. She arched a brow, seeming to contemplate Holly's mental state. "I'm talking about the new owner. He has a tendency to wander the halls at night. Occupational hazard."

"Ghost hunter?" Holly supplied, hiding her smile.

Charlotte ignored her, nodding to the phone on a table next to the four-poster bed. "If you need anything he'll take care of you. You may help yourself to anything in the kitchen, but the third floor is restricted access."

Nothing said haunted house like part of it being off limits. "The vampire's domain?"

With a hurried nod, Charlotte stepped into the hall. She withdrew something from her pocket and pressed it into Holly's hand. "Keep this close."

Holly studied the folded-leather, recognizing the gris-gris, a Voodoo charm.

Nice touch.

Charlotte hesitated. "I hope you're everything he thinks you are."

Well that explained the woman's attitude. Charlotte must not have approved of the owner agreeing to use Beau Arbor House in her article.

"Good night." Before closing the door, Charlotte's expression softened a fraction. "If you need someone to talk to later, you can find me in the small house at the rear of the property."

Ooookay.

Alone in the room, Holly put the odd housekeeper out of her mind and set her overnight bag and laptop case on the bench at the foot of the bed.

She caught a glance at herself in the mirror across the room. She immediately ran her hands through her hair in an effort to detangle the mess of auburn curls that were about to frizz out. Faint shadows lingered beneath her green eyes, but at least she wasn't having problems sleeping anymore.

With her coat off, she finally started warming up. A hot shower would take care of the rest. Or a bath, she quickly amended, discovering the gorgeous claw-foot tub in the bathroom that she thankfully didn't have to share with any other guests on the floor.

First, though, she was starving and in serious need of a drink. She felt too on edge and suspected that had nothing to do with haunted houses and everything to do with being back in New Orleans.

Ruthlessly shoving aside memories of her last time here, she retraced her steps back to the main floor, pausing halfway down the last staircase. The fiddle music played from above now, though she hadn't heard the music pass her room.

Another staircase at the back of the house. Right?

Holly nearly laughed at herself. The woman's whole performance about spirits had not unsettled her.

A sound burst from her pocket and she nearly tripped off the last stair, heart-thundering.

"God damn it," she breathed, pulling her phone out of her pocket and checking the caller ID. Lena.

Deciding she'd give Lena an update after she'd had something to eat and looked around, she let the call go to voicemail.

The fiddle music followed her into the kitchen. While the rest of the house had been restored to its 18th century glory, the kitchen had been completely modernized, complete with stainless steel appliances and granite countertops.

The lights had been left on, making it easy to spot the glass-covered dish of cookies and beignets in the middle of the island. Extra plates had been set next to the serving dish, and once she grabbed a couple of each treat and snagged a bottle of wine and glass, she turned to leave.

Movement from the corner of her eye should have prepared her.

She screamed anyway, jumping away from the man who rounded the corner and nearly knocked her off her feet. She managed to keep a grip on the wine, but the plate, along with beignets and cookies, didn't survive.

"Crap." Holly crouched to pick up the chunks of shattered glass and cookies. "At least I didn't throw it at you. I've done worse when someone scared me."

"I've got the scars to prove it."

Rich, sensual, and achingly familiar...

Holly fell back on her butt, staring up through another tangle of hair at the man hovering over her.

Not just another guest. Not a ghost either, and when faced with the reality of the situation, she would have preferred a close encounter of the phantom kind.

"Sam?" Her voice came out sounding like someone had stepped on her windpipe.

Sam Reeves. Writer, lover—heartbreaker.

All six feet of him crouched opposite her, his rumpled red t-shirt straining across his shoulders and chest and looking like he might have fallen asleep at his desk again. Dark brown hair in need of a haircut fell across his forehead, and intense chocolate brown eyes locked her in place.

"The scar is more disfiguring than you remember, isn't it?"

Holly blinked, her gaze sliding to the hairline scar near his left eyebrow that she'd given him two months ago when he'd jumped out of a closet at her. She'd been carrying her laptop at the time and it took less damage than his head. The ten-stitch injury had been covered with a bandage the last time she'd seen him.

The last time she'd been in New Orleans.

"What are you doing here?" Although Sam looked just as stunned to see her, the emotionless question cut nearly as deep as his departure from her life, wiping out dozens of memories that could have made her do something stupid—like launch herself straight into his arms.

Deep breath. Deep...breath.

Her pulse refused to settle as she concentrated on cleaning up the mess so she didn't have to look at him. "Fuck a duck." The muttered curse didn't make her feel any better.

"What was that?"

She heard the smile in his voice, but it only stoked the anger brewing inside her. The unexpected emotion eroded the shock at finding herself face to face with the man who broke her heart.

"I stopped by your room, but you weren't there."

Her head snapped up. "You knew I was here?"

He nodded, carrying the broken plate to the garbage can. "I never thought you'd actually come. Figured you'd cancel once you knew..." he trailed off, his brows drawing together. "You didn't know, did you?" He stopped opposite her.

"You arranged this?" He'd left messages before, though not for a few weeks, but she wouldn't have imagined he'd pull something like this.

Sam's hand closed around hers, and her eyes nearly slid shut at the tingling warmth that spread across her skin.

Then she remembered how mad she was, how devastated she'd been.

"So no one gets hurt." That heartbreaking smile was back in his voice, and she glanced at the hand that gently pried the largest chunk of broken glass from her fingers, then met his eyes.

He set the glass on the counter, then took the bottle of wine from her as well. "I'd rather not play the odds."

"Thinking about hiding the knives too?"

He shrugged. "Frying pans are closer. I'm assuming you'd go for those first."

She resisted the urge to look over her shoulder in search of them. "You don't sound surprised."

"I'm sure I deserve worse."

Worse was a lot like calling a category 5 hurricane a tropical storm.

Her phone rang again, and to escape the intensity of his gaze without looking like she was avoiding it, she dug it out of her pocket and checked the caller ID. Lena again. When she let it go to voicemail only to have Lena call right back, she glanced back and forth between the ringing phone and Sam's guarded expression.

"You called Lena."

He didn't look the least bit apologetic about it. "You wouldn't answer my calls."

"You left without a word." Without a goddamn word.

She'd left him in her New Orleans hotel room after spending the most incredible week with him, and when she returned with breakfast, intending to fall back into bed with him, he was gone.

Stunned, she'd been unable to reach him until she'd returned home, the need for an explanation for the unexpected disappearance eating away at her. Had he lied about being a widow? Did he really have a wife at home, or a girlfriend?

Sam's dismissive explanation, that they'd had a

great time together and that it was fun while it lasted, had stung more than if he had been a cheating scumbag. She'd cried for way too long, reliving the moments they'd lain together laughing until they couldn't breathe, the protective way he'd slept holding onto her, like she might be ripped away from him at any moment, the slow trace of his fingers across her cheek when she woke each morning.

She'd cried, called herself naïve and every kind of fool she could think of, then finally pulled herself together.

But 'fun while it fucking lasted'? Remembering the brief conversation made the nerves in her stomach snap and crackle like vegetation caught in a brush fire.

"You said...forget it." She had. Had forced herself to forget everything about him.

Or so she'd thought. Ten seconds in his presence and she could remember far too much. The smell of his cologne without tucking his face against his neck. The sound of his laugh and the goofy way he'd wiggle his eyebrows when he was trying to make her smile.

And worst of all, she could remember the way he kissed her, the slow slide of his bottom lip across hers, and the teasing nip with his teeth before he knocked her whole world sideways with his mouth.

"I'm sorry."

"You said that before." Right before he'd crushed her heart under his boot heel, and she'd let it happen.

Somehow she'd let herself fall in love with him after only a week affair, convincing herself that all their laughter and conversations into the middle of the night had meant something.

That she had meant something to him.

"I am sorry," Sam insisted, sounding too much like the distant man who'd all but told her to have a nice life two months ago.

She might have been tempted to take a swing at him with the wine bottle if she thought it would make her feel less like a sucker for believing his feelings for her were genuine.

Sam watched Holly's gaze land on the wine bottle and instinctively nudged it a little further out of reach.

Until ten minutes ago, he'd been convinced she wouldn't come, had expected at least one phone call to tell him off. As much as he'd wanted to believe no phone calls were a good sign, he hadn't dared to get his hopes up.

And here she was.

So close he could reach out and trace the splash of freckles across her nose, could slip his palm around the nape of her neck and slide perfectly into her personal space...

If she wasn't staring at him like she might skip the frying pans and go right for the knives after all.

This wasn't going well.

Charlotte had warned him that Holly might still be angry, that any woman had the right to be furious at him for playing the ultimate asshole card—love'em and leave'em. Charlotte had never met Holly before tonight and she'd still raked him over the coals weeks ago when he'd owned up to the real reason he'd walked away.

He'd been terrified.

Down to the wire editorial deadlines, rabid critics, hell, even the twisted psychopaths he wrote about—were he to face one of his fictional villains—were nothing compared to loving and trusting someone the way he wanted to with Holly.

After seven days together, seven days of aching to spend more time with her than he had anyone else, he'd made the colossal mistake of getting the hell out of there.

And then spent the next seven weeks regretting every second of it.

"I didn't mean what I said."

"You mentioned that." She stuffed her phone back in her pocket. "In a message you left on my voicemail. When you were drinking."

"Drunk actually," he admitted, then winced at just how bad it sounded aloud.

She whistled. "Wow. You're racking up the brownie points now."

"Is that why you didn't call me back?" He'd passed out that night with the phone on the pillow next to him, half wishing he might find her there instead when he woke up.

Holly's expression softened, then she crossed her arms, keeping a wall up between them. "Even I'm not dumb enough to take drunk dialing seriously."

"It wasn't like that." All of the words he'd rehearsed in his head in the days since he'd reached out for Lena's help had fled, leaving him stumbling the same way he had the night they met.

"So you didn't drunk dial me?"

Drunk might have been an understatement, but he was already treading on dangerous ground so he kept that to himself. "I called because I needed to hear the sound of your voice."

Holly's eyes lost some of their hostility, the first sign that maybe he stood half a chance repairing the damage he'd done.

Without a word, she swiveled around on her heel and walked out of the room.

"Shit." He braced his hands on the counter, wondering if he'd made a mistake bringing her here instead of being at her place, waiting for her when she got home from her trip.

"Wait." He followed her.

Holly never made it past the front parlor, her gaze locked on the bottle of wine sitting in the middle of the bottom step.

She swung back around, retraced her steps and checked the kitchen to confirm what he already knew— that it was the same bottle of wine he'd set on the counter.

"I think we're past the point of selling me on the haunted house, don't you?" She ignored the bottle with only the slightest pause, as if she had to tell herself it was really just a trick, and then carried on.

He didn't let her get too far ahead of him.

Halfway up, she glanced back, not all that surprised that he was right on her heels. "Could you kindly tell the fiddle player that this isn't the Grand Ole Opry?"

Accustomed to the nightly music, Sam could only shrug.

"Please thank Charlotte for waiting around for me and that I'm sorry for the broken dish." She walked into her room then spun around at the last second, like she was about to close the door in his face, but slammed into his chest instead.

On reflex he caught her around the waist, keeping her in his arms, exactly where he'd spent countless nights imagining her. Her gaze slid up to meet his, pausing on his lips just long enough to make him forget where they were, and whatever the hell they'd been talking about.

It seemed important, but with Holly so soft and warm and tucked so sweetly against him, simple brain function was a challenge. No other women had ever reduced him to such a complete tongue-tied, lust-filled moron, and he'd forgotten how accustomed he'd grown to that sensation whenever she was around.

The hungry ache inside him drew his attention straight to her mouth, and he lifted a hand, eager to smooth his palm across her cheek.

"Where's my stuff?"

It took about three seconds too long to get his mind off how badly he wanted her naked and beneath him, and another two to process that she was definitely not on the same page he was. It was a safe bet they weren't even reading from the same book.

Without sacrificing his hold on her entirely, he moved them further into the room. He gave the room a cursory sweep, not bothering to check under the bed or the closet for the bags he'd seen on her bed a while ago.

"That would be Oscar."

Her brows scrunched together. "The loud one?"

"Charlotte warned you about Oscar?" Beau Arbor's housekeeper preferred not to rile their permanent guests by talking about them, which had always annoyed Sam's aunt. Haunted houses couldn't make money if the staff refused to talk about it.

Holly's gorgeous green eyes flared. "Too bad she didn't warn me about you."

Thunking footsteps echoed in the hall, saving him from defending his actions again.

She glanced at the door. "Would that be Oscar?"

"Undoubtedly."

She frowned at the grip he had on her hand, but didn't shake him off. Either she realized he had no intention of letting her go or didn't mind it so much. He hoped like hell it was the latter.

She poked her head into the hall. "There's no one there."

"Yeah, that's sort of his thing."

Holly shot him a sharp glance, tinged with disbelief. He wasn't getting into it now, though. He had his hands full convincing her to give him another chance, let alone explaining about Oscar. He should have been prepared for the luggage to go missing, though. It was Oscar's typical MO.

"I screwed up, Holly. I never meant what I said—"

She cut him off. "Which part? That it was fun or nice knowing me?"

He flinched at the poorly chosen words he'd used to get her off the phone before he begged her to come back. "I don't think I put it quite that way."

She glared at him.

"It was stupid." So fucking stupid. "I panicked and screwed up."

He hadn't planned on ever meeting anyone like her. Smart and sexy and sweet...he'd been convinced he couldn't possibly deserve her. He'd loved someone once and lost her, but none of that prepared him for how deeply and how quickly he'd fallen for Holly.

"Really? And did you figure that out before or after I all but begged to see you again and you said it wasn't a good time for you?"

Hurt laced her words, slicing him to the bone. It had been the worst time imaginable, and although he'd figured out by then just how much he needed her in his life, he'd refused to let her come.

"My aunt was sick," he began.

She shook her head, not wanting to hear it. "You know what? It doesn't matter. It's over with."

"Holly, please."

"No, you were right. You had your life here and I had mine. Long distance relationships never last."

"I never wanted that." He could never have settled for just seeing her every other weekend or once a month.

"And you made that perfectly clear two months ago."

He blew out a breath, scrambling for a way to fix this. "You get that I was an idiot, right?"

"Was? You think it's okay to interfere in my life this way? To call my boss and sell her on a haunted house because you were looking for a booty call?"

It was the absolute worst reaction to have, but he couldn't help himself—he burst out laughing.

Holly's cheeks turned pink. She shook off his hand and stalked to the door. "You need to leave."

Angry or not, she was the most amazing thing he'd seen in years. "I didn't try to get you here for a booty call."

"So you don't want to have sex with me?"

He studied her face, sensing some kind of trap. "There is no right answer to that question."

She folded her arms across her chest. Waiting for him to leave, or explain himself? He went with the latter.

"If I say no, that I don't want to get you naked, you might think that I'm not attracted enough or something equally crazy. Or worse, that I'm trying to get you naked to fix the situation."

"And you're not?"

He took a step toward her, not stopping until only inches separated them. "If I thought I could make everything okay between us with sex, I would've had you up against the car in the pouring rain the second you got here."

Her eyes locked on his, drawing out the moment. She let out a slow breath. "So you do want sex."

He waited, wondering if there was an accusation buried in there somewhere. "Absofuckinglutely."

Her lips parted, but he didn't give her the chance to interrupt.

He tipped her face up, needing to be sure she wouldn't look away and tune him out. "We need to talk. I know that. And I know that you need time to process this. But I won't lie and say that I haven't thought of having you in my bed a hundred times a day in a hundred different ways since I walked away from you."

Pushing his luck, Sam lowered his head until his lips hovered above her cheek. He could still smell the rain on her skin and wanted nothing more than to peel off her wet clothes and feel her warmth against him.

Which was exactly why he released her and stepped back into the doorway instead. And it fucking killed him to do it.

"I'll be upstairs. Possibly taking a cold shower." And likely booking a flight to follow her home if she left without giving him a chance to explain everything. He would do whatever he had to, to convince her to take a chance on him—hopefully without looking like a stalker from one of his books. "But please don't leave. Not while you're mad at me."

"I stopped being angry at you a long time ago."

"Liar," he said softly. He wasn't even done being mad at himself yet. It shouldn't have taken days to realize that the only place he needed to be was with Holly. Instead he'd pulled away, convinced himself their week together hadn't been that big of a deal.

If it hadn't been for his aunt, for the leukemia that took her far too soon, would he have realized what he'd nearly given up with Holly?

He retreated into the hall.

Anger and confusion darkened Holly's eyes. "Why should I wait?"

74

He paused. "Aside from the fact that your luggage is missing?"

She cocked her head, and for a second he could have sworn the corner of her lips twitched.

"Fiery, intelligent eyes. Hair up, but falling down because you couldn't stop tugging on the loose strands. Short black dress, like charcoal painted on your skin and showing off enough cleavage to make every man in the place wish they were standing as close to you as I was. Feet bare, your shoes underneath your stool at the bar. No jewelry and more pink lip gloss on your hurricane glass than on your lips."

"That was the—"

"The night we met." He shoved his hands in his pockets, struggling to make the right choice, and not the selfish one by simply kissing her until she saw things the way he did. "The best night of my life."

Then he turned and walked down the hall, hoping like hell he hadn't dropped the ball for the second time.

On auto-pilot, Holly shut the door, and because her knees were shaking so badly, she sat on the edge of the bed.

Outside the shelter of the room, rain pelted the French doors leading to the private balcony and wind rattled the frame with the force of a rising storm.

Fitting.

Though she sat perfectly still, her insides teetered on the edge of a whirlwind. One step back and maybe she could keep all the pieces holding her together intact.

One step forward...

Screw it.

Holly was across the room and down the hall so quickly she nearly missed the staircase to the third floor.

Ignoring the heavy footsteps and fiddle music, she jogged up the steps before she could ask herself if she was out of her mind.

Movement in a room she passed snagged her attention and she backtracked to find Sam in a home office. His?

He would have heard her coming up the steps, but he didn't look up from the fireplace where the flames had nearly gone out.

"That's the second time you've walked out on me."

He glanced at her, the pain and regret in his eyes nearly taking her breath. She was intimately familiar with sexy Sam and laughing and joking Sam, along with mildly annoyed, curious, and far too serious.

But vulnerable? Not so much. So attentive and strong and cocky, and a little bit...lost.

Between one breath and the next every feeling for him she'd so intentionally buried crashed through the surface, nearly unraveling her where she stood.

"There's nothing that will undo the hurt, is there?"

Holly shook her head. What's done, was done. Nothing he said or did could take back the moments when she would have ripped out her own heart just to make it stop hurting.

She'd been swept away the second he hit on here in the hotel bar with a cheesy pickup line. She'd felt such strength in his arms and love. He'd never said the words, but she'd read them in his eyes, tasted them in every kiss.

And then told herself, convinced herself, she'd been horribly wrong.

But she hadn't been, had she? The doubt that swirled inside her faded with every second he stood there looking like he'd walk through fire for her.

Or was she being naïve all over again?"

She shook her head. "You don't get to say that stuff." His brows creased together, but she kept going. "You don't get to say that, to remember the night we met even better than I do, and then walk away without…" She took a breath, her heart hammering in her chest.

"Holly?"

"Without kissing me," she finished, the words ending on a whisper.

Sam didn't wait for her to get all the words out, and she was in his arms.

Just one minute, she promised herself. One minute to lose herself in him, to drown in the sheer pleasure of his touch, whether he was kissing her until she couldn't breathe or hunting for the perfect ticklish spot.

Just one minute to ruin any chance she had of forgetting him for good.

"Holly," he breathed, her name on his lips sending a sun-warmed shiver sliding down her spine.

And then he sealed his mouth over hers.

One minute would never be enough. Maybe not even one lifetime. Not when she was melting into him, diving headlong over the edge with only the arms dragging her impossibly close to hold onto.

His tongue pushed past her lips, seeking and claiming in one possessive sweep. She moaned at the pure carnal heat tunneling through her blood, marking her like a brand.

But far more sabotaging was the emotion swelling inside her, making her curl her fingers even tighter around the t-shirt gathered in her hands.

God, how she wanted this to be real. For the both of them.

"You're here." Two tiny words whispered against her hair between Sam's breaths, between taking complete possession of her mouth, and the tension coiled insider her snapped.

She caged his face in her hands. "You really want this? Want to be with me."

"With you is the only place I'll ever want to be."

"But you left." No matter how good it felt in his arms, she couldn't let herself forget that.

"I made a mistake. The biggest of my life. After Selene died, I never wanted to care that much for anyone, let alone fall even harder for someone else."

"You love me?" The words trembled out, her instinct to believe him at war with the need to protect herself.

Sam nodded, his brown eyes so probing and intense, and holding back nothing.

"Then I really don't understand."

A tentative smile teased his mouth. "I freaked out, told myself that week with you was just a fluke. That I couldn't handle any more complications. And really, I was just so..."

"Full of crap?" she provided, feeling like smiling for the first time. "You never said any of this on the phone."

"By the time I told myself not to be such a chickenshit, I was needed here."

She thought of Charlotte's comment about being in mourning. "Your aunt got sick," she repeated, remembering what he'd tried to tell her earlier.

Sadness crept into his face.

"She's gone, isn't she?"

His slow nod tugged her heart until she was sure it couldn't take any more tonight. "I miss her a lot. She would have liked you." He pushed a few strands of hair behind her ear.

"And this was the house you talked about having to

leave New York to visit every summer growing up? But you joked about it being haunted…" She trailed off, frowning.

"I believe you already met Oscar."

Her eyes widened. "You weren't joking, were you?"

"Unfortunately not. They grow on you, though."

She glanced around the room, skepticism narrowing her eyes. "Oscar is one of the confederate soldiers I read about on the website?"

"You get used to him and William."

"Is he the fiddle player?" She lowered her voice, half wondering if even asking the question would make it somehow real.

Sam laughed, the sound heady and intoxicating, and the only thing that might make her forget the whole idea of Beau Arbor House actually being haunted.

"We'll talk about them later." He kissed her again, slowly, a teasing slide of his mouth across hers. "I need you to tell me that we can do this. Be together. You can stay here as long as you want or I'll go wherever you want me to."

"And when you get sick of me?"

"Never gonna happen."

"Because you love me." The more she said it, the more right it felt.

"Because I don't want to go another minute knowing what it's like to live without you."

"Sam—" she began.

He shook his head, silencing the doubts that cautioned her not to fall so easily a second time. "I know it's a lot to take in. Just give it some time. Give us some time."

If she was wrong…

"I won't hurt you again, Holly. Just stay with me. Please." His mouth closed over hers once more, wickedly soft and melting her resistance faster than snowflakes caught in the rain.

"Okay."

He smiled against her lips. "You should know that I really want to get to the part where you're naked in my bed."

"Your ghosts aren't going to watch, are they?" she teased.

"Don't let the door hit you on the way out, Oscar."

She raised her hand to punch Sam in the arm just as the office door slammed shut.

"And they're trapped here?"

It was the third time Holly had run him through the story of Beau Arbor's haunting past, and Sam didn't mind even a little bit. It helped that her amazing naked body was sprawled across his chest and he could content himself with running his hand up and down her back as they talked.

He'd woken half a dozen times throughout the night, awed by the sight of her asleep next to him. Only once had she opened her eyes and noticed him watching her.

Sleepy-eyed, she had snuggled closer and teasingly warned, "You've got two months to make up for, Sam. You're going to need your sleep."

He'd laughed and rolled her beneath him. "Then I'd best get started."

Thinking about the hours he'd spent reacquainting himself with her body and the sounds she made when he kissed, licked and tasted every inch of her, only managed to get him fired up all over again.

Although he wanted her again—always wanted her—he ignored his increasing arousal, focusing on Holly's recounting.

She propped her chin on her hands. "Two brothers in love with the same woman. They go off to war. The youngest deserts right before the end of the conflict, intent on declaring his love, only to realize she really is in love with his brother, Oscar. And though his heart was broken, William stays with her when she gets sick and develops a fever."

"He took care of her the way Oscar would have. William felt he owed his brother that much." Sam knew Holly would have a clearer understanding when she read William's journal.

"Then right after she dies, Oscar returns wounded and dies of an infection less than a week later. And if that's not tragic enough, William contracts the same fever that killed the woman they both adored, and dies himself." Her eyes glistened. "It's so sad."

"Losing people you love is hard."

Holly glanced up at him. "Do you think your aunt's ghost is here too?"

"Not that I've noticed. Better for William and Oscar that way. The woman was a tyrant."

"You loved that tyrant." She lowered her eyes. "I wish you would have told me when she was sick. I would have come."

"I wasn't so sure you would. And to be honest, as much as I would have loved that, I loved spending those last few weeks with her. Even if she spent half the time bitching about the music or Oscar keeping her up at night."

Although she'd heard the music and footsteps throughout the night and had discovered her bags had been returned without Sam leaving her sight, her rational, journalistic mind struggled to make sense of everything.

He couldn't blame her. If he hadn't spent summers here growing up, he would be just as skeptical and determined to explain the unexplainable.

"Now that the history lesson is complete, I believe it's time to move on to a lesson in anatomy." Sam tugged the sheet down, watching the white cotton slowly reveal the curves of her breasts.

Laughing, she tried to squirm free, only to still the moment he ran his mouth down her throat.

Footsteps echoed in the hall.

"Again?" Growling, Holly rolled away from him and slipped out of the bed.

"It's a waste of time." He cocked his head, enjoying the view of her phenomenal ass as she stalked to the door.

"I've had enough of the stomping up and down the hall."

"It's morning," he tried to warn her, then recognizing that she didn't care what he thought, he relaxed back on the pillow to watch the show.

Holly wrenched the door open, "Ghost or not, you really need to stop skulking up and down—"

"Good morning to you too, Ms. Clarke." Charlotte stood in the hallway.

Holly shrieked, turned and dove back into the bed, nearly ripping the sheet off him in her attempt to cover herself up.

Salvaging little more than a fistful of the sheet to keep himself from becoming the star of the show, he glanced at the housekeeper. "Did you need something Charlie?"

Not the least bit concerned that he was three cubic inches from a fully monty, his housekeeper set a tray with the newspaper and two cups of coffee on the chair closest to the door. "Should I assume this means breakfast for two?"

"Yes."

Her lips twitched. "And she'll be staying with us for a while?"

A muffled, "Yes," came from the woman hiding beneath the sheet.

As soon as the door closed, Holly punched him in the arm. "You could have warned me."

He grinned at her.

She narrowed her eyes. "You knew it was her in the hall."

"I had my suspicions."

A get-even glimmer lit up her eyes. "You're gonna pay for that. Slowly. Painfully." She tugged at the corner of the sheet covering him.

Heat flared through him, but before she could lower her head and begin the best kind of torture he could think of, he dragged her up his body. Her lips were still curved in a smile when he coaxed her down to meet his mouth.

He couldn't imagine a better start to the rest of their lives.

Laissez les Bons Temps Rouler *by Juniper Bell*

"Laaaaiiiiisssssezzz les boooonnnnnn …" A cat in heat, that's what it sounded like to Arrietta. A wild, rutting, howling cat on a hot tin roof. Except this caterwauling demon was strutting across a stage, not a roof, and that stage happened to be in the bar next door on Frenchmen's Street. Which wouldn't be a problem except that she was trying to sing too. Her rendition of "Blue Collar Boogie" kept getting drowned out by the ridiculous screeching next door, and her overflow crowd of twenty—make that eighteen—seemed to be overflowing right out the door.

She sang louder. "Some say work is good for the soul …" Her voice cracked. Josh, on standup bass, made a face at her. She flared her nostrils at him. He crinkled his forehead in a way that gave her a funny little twinge and made her stumble over the next word. "… but I see … say … I sold my soul forty hours a week." She shot Josh a glare, only to be deafened by another blast of sound from next door.

"…roulllleeeerrr! Yow!!! Come on, pretty mama!"

"You've got to be kidding!" With a squeal of feedback, Arrietta yanked the mike out of its stand. "Can't someone do something?"

Josh and Mackie D, her drummer, stumbled to a stop, the music crashing around them like a building in mid-demolition. With a quizzical look, Josh tilted his derby hat further back on his head. Mackie D just stared at her, his big black bulk solid as a mountain behind his drum set. They'd been playing together as Miss Jess for two years in Brooklyn, and were just starting to get some notice.

Arrietta had slaved for this day. She'd gone into debt, she'd lived in shithole apartments her entire adult life, done all her shopping at Goodwill. She'd worked as a waitress, a psychic hotline operator, even a secretarial temp to pay the bills. She'd sacrificed everything – friendships, romances, financial security—for her music.

Sure, sometimes she wished she could just let it rip, like that loudmouth good ol' boy next door. Forget technique, forget lessons and scales. But she'd hadn't spent all those years mastering her craft to let Miss Jess's all-important first gig in New Orleans—on Valentine's Day, no less—get ruined by a jackass.

She leaned back into the mike and breathed, "We'll be back in five." With one more annoyed look at her do-nothing bandmates, she stalked off the stage.

Blank, astonished faces watched her progress through Hurricane City and out the door. No one seemed too concerned about the racket next door. Maybe they were used to this in New Orleans—one group completely drowning out another. Well, Arrietta hadn't paid her dues in the Brooklyn music scene for nothing. Maybe other singers didn't mind straining their vocal chords to be heard over a screeching banshee, but she wasn't going to put up with it for one more second.

The bar next door was called "Chez le Voodoo". It had an annoyingly vintage New Orleans look about it, with ornate gold lettering and a dim interior that seemed to be lit by gas lamps. An impassive man sat on a stool outside the front door. He looked her up and down, then back up, then back down.

She thought she looked pretty good, with her hair in pink, marcelled waves, like a fifties pin-up. In honor of Valentine's Day, she'd added a fascinator with a sparkly heart. Her onstage style was tongue-in-cheek retro, with a poodle skirt that had been altered to feature a wildcat rather than a poodle, and a halter top that showed off the tattoo of an eyelash-batting kitten on her upper back. But the bouncer didn't seem impressed. He held out his hand, palm up.

"I'm not staying," she told him. "I'm singing next door and I need to talk to someone about the sound level."

When he didn't lower his hand, she rolled her eyes and reached into her cleavage. With a quick glance to make sure it wasn't one of her twenties, she slapped it into his hand. He grunted and waved her in.

Bedlam, that's what it was. As she stepped into Chez le Voodoo, an absolutely wild scene unfurled before her. The walls were black, as if decades of smoke had infused every crack in the wood. Every few feet, flames danced and leaped inside glass wall sconces. The place was so packed, Arrietta couldn't even make out where the bar was. Couples were romping and whooping; some were executing tight spins and dips and whirls. Fragrant cigarette smoke curled through the air as if the place were an opium den. Arrietta tossed her head, ignoring the seductive pull of all that wild abandon. Talk about old skool. A lot of bars didn't even allow smoking anymore.

But clearly, Chez le Voodoo followed its own rules.

Indecent exposure, for example.

She peered into the smoky crowd. The flickering gas lamps acted as a sort of old-fashioned strobe light, so she could see only in flashes. But she was pretty sure … yes, practically positive … that some of the women were dancing topless.

Well, it was New Orleans, after all. But she'd thought that sort of thing was saved for the tourists down on Bourbon Street. This was Frenchmen's Street, where all the serious music lovers went. And she was a Serious Musician—on a mission.

She swung her gaze to the stage, where she spotted the cause of her outrage.

There he was, the devil who'd been ruining her set. He stood with legs apart, hands gripping a saxophone, lips wrapped around the mouthpiece. At least he wasn't singing at the moment, but his sax playing was just as bad. The man had no technique whatsoever. He just threw notes out there as if they were cheap Mardi Gras beads. Fast and raw, the notes scampered up and down the scale. The dancing crowd gyrated right along with the madman, faster and faster, as if they'd all die if they stopped—or even slowed down.

Then he pulled the sax out of his mouth and yanked the mike to his lips. And Arrietta came close to fainting. The man was … what were the right words? He was like some kind of god—the pagan kind. He had black hair, thick as blackstrap molasses, with a shiver of black stubble on his jaw. His eyes glittered like midnight swamp water, like alligators sidling alongside bayou skiffs, like wild Southern belles throwing tossing up their skirts on a hot summer night. Every naughty thought, every dangerous, spontaneous impulse gleamed in those eyes. And every woman in the place knew it.

"Laiiiiiissssezzzz les …."

And those broad shoulders, hunched over the mike as if he was making sweet, sweet love to it. His lean hips thrust in time to the beat. Tendons stood out in his neck. Sweat dripped down his face. The man was sex. Pure sex on a mike stand.

But he still couldn't sing.

Arrietta steeled herself and marched through the crowd to the edge of the stage. "Hey, mister!" She called to the singer, tilting her head back.

Lost in his crazy caterwauling, he ignored her completely.

"Hey you!"

He swept the mike stand across the stage as if it were a dance partner. But he still didn't seem to hear her.

Fine. If he was going to play it this way, she'd have to get serious. She opened her mouth and let out a long, penetrating high C, the note no one else in her class at Juilliard had been able to hit.

"Shuuuuuut uuuuup!" She sang. The wall sconces rattled. The cymbals quivered. Even the cigarette smoke seemed to shiver.

And abruptly, her voice was the only sound in the place. All the singing stopped, along with every riff from the back-up band. The dancing stopped, as if everyone was suddenly frozen in place.

Arrietta swallowed hard. Miffed as she'd been, she hadn't wanted to ruin the party completely. "A little softer, please," she ventured. The singer's deep, dark gaze swung toward her, and for a crazy moment she knew that if she didn't leave now, it would swallow her whole. "I'm trying to sing next door," she finished, with an awkward gesture toward the front door. "I'm … uh … here from Brooklyn. With my band. We're a trio. Kind of a blues-rockabilly-swing fusion." Too much information? Yeah. Definitely. She turned to go. "Okay, thanks bye! Carry on. Just not too loud."

By the time she reached the front door, she was practically running. The warm, neon-tinted night air of Frenchmen's Street greeted her as she burst out the front door. The expressionless bouncer showed equally little reaction to her departure as he had to her arrival. She hurried back to Hurricane City, where the crowd, which had gotten even smaller, was listening to Josh and Mackie D pick out an old Cab Calloway tune.

"That's better," she muttered to Josh as she made her way onto the stage.

"Are you all right?" he whispered. Trust Josh to think first about her welfare. He was a sweetheart down to the bone. Cute, too. Not sex god cute like the singer at Chez le Voodoo, but cute enough to keep her up at night, wondering why she'd instituted the no-relationship rule for the band.

But she knew very well why. Because she'd been burned one too many times and knew better. The last time Josh had asked her out, she'd been brutally honest and told him she'd never go out with another musician again. Musicians were nothing but trouble. She didn't need trouble.

"I will be if we can finish this set so people can actually hear me." Why did he look so puzzled? Surely he too must be relieved that the dreadful cacophony from next door had stopped. "Blue Collar Boogie, from the top." Maybe they could actually complete a song before Cajun Sex God started up again.

No such luck. As soon as the bass notes of the intro had passed and she opened her mouth, the singing next door began again.

Twice as loud.

"Laiiiiiisssssez les Bon Temps ..."

"Fuck him and his fucking crappy-ass singing!" Arrietta blurted into the mike.

"Arrietta!" Josh's shocked voice sounded behind her.

"I don't care! This is fucking bullshit!" She threw aside the mike and stormed off the stage. "I'll be right back."

This time she was ready with a handful of dollar bills, which she slapped into the bouncer's hand. This time the crazy scene inside Chez le Voodoo didn't slow her down a bit as she stalked onto the stage. Not even the sight of the lead singer's bare chest, revealed by the shirt he'd ripped open, slowed her down—although every detail of his darkly furred chest and hard muscles registered in her brain.

She marched across the stage until she reached the singer, who still hadn't noticed her. For some reason this infuriated her more than anything. Taking him by surprise, she yanked the mike away from him.

"Do you really call this music?" she railed at him. "If you ask me, it's just a bunch of noise!"

A lazy smile quirked the corner of his mouth as he gave her a cocked-head once-over. "And you are, cher?" His accent was thick and Cajun, like warmed honey poured over flapjacks.

"Arrietta Hammond," she answered, ignoring the better judgment that told her not to reveal too much. "Juilliard graduate and winner of the Jazz Songstress of the Year Award in 2008."

"2008, eh?" A funny look, almost regretful, crossed his face. "Tres bien, you."

God, it was hot up on this stage. No wonder the man had ripped off his shirt. Her eyes drifted to his sternum, then to the dark patch of curly hair on his muscled chest. She thought she saw an odd shadow on his belly, but when she blinked, it was gone. And she realized she'd been staring just a little too long for politeness.

"Yeah, well, that was a while ago. And my career hasn't exactly gone the way I thought it would since then. But I'm here now, and I'd really appreciate the chance to share my music with the people of New Orleans." Or at least fifteen of them, at last count.

"So, ma petite beignet, you bring your magic to Frenchmen's street, eh ben? Vas-y, cher. Show us what you got dere." He gestured to the mike.

"Oh no. I'm not here to sing. My band's waiting for me at Hurricane City. I just came to ask you if you could turn it down a notch." She remembered that this was her second trip to the Voodoo. "I asked you before but it didn't seem to do much good."

He shrugged. "I have no control over dis. The music, she do what she do."

"Maybe you should consider voice lessons. Vocal control is an important element for any singer."

Amusement flashed across his voice. "Control, you say? Is dis hard to learn?"

She peered at him suspiciously. "Are you making fun of me?" She glanced behind them at the band, who were all leaning on their instruments, looking positively gleeful.

"And if I do? My daddy always say, nothing wrong with a little fun. Isn't dat what it's all about?"

"What what's all about?"

"Dis!" He made an expansive gesture around the room. The crowd didn't appear to be disturbed by the interruption. They'd mostly turned back to their hurricanes and their flirtations. Some were still dancing. "Everyone is here for a little fun, no?"

"See? There's your problem." She pointed at him triumphantly. "You're not taking any of this seriously. You act like it's all a big joke. I'm trying to make a career here. I worked really hard to make this album. I came all the way here from Brooklyn to play these songs. You probably...I don't know, maybe you play only on weekends with your buddies. My life...my entire life...is music. It's not a joke to me." She ended on an impassioned note that shocked even her. Her voice squeaked to a stop. So much for vocal control.

"Then why do you not sing for us, cher? We love music too, I guar-on-tee. If you sing it, they will come." Again he indicated the crowd with a sweep of his arm. "And a better audience, you won't find anywhere on heaven or earth. Or down below." He winked. "And my band will follow a true chanteuse to the ends of the earth. Allez, ma petite beignet!"

For the first time, she seriously considered the idea. This crowd was a lot bigger than the one next door. "Why do you keep calling me that?"

"Because you are so plump and sugary that I want to eat you up."

As his gaze slid across her, a lush sort of sensual confidence followed in its wake. Normally she thought about her appearance only enough to put together an outfit for her performance. Style and presentation were important to a female singer, everyone knew that. She had to project a certain amount of sex appeal. But it was only on the surface; inside she was all business.

But the way he was looking at her with those sinfully black eyes made something spark to life inside her. Talk about sex appeal—this man exuded sex from every pore of his body, without any sort of effort. It came from inside, from the relaxed way he moved, the way he talked, the way he took his time looking at her.

As if trying to become worthy of such a look, her body went liquid and lazy inside. She felt her lips curve into a provocative smile that her brain hadn't intended to produce.

"Ah, now that's more like it. Now our petite beignet is having fun. When's the last time you had a good laugh, cher?"

"I laugh all the time." With Josh, she added silently. Josh could make her laugh with nothing more than a comical lift of his eyebrow.

"Do you now? And when's the last time you had a good fuck?"

"What?"

"A fuck. A romp. A roll in de hay. A dip in the swamp. A dance between the bedposts." He looked as if he'd have no problem coming up with a hundred new phrases to describe one simple act.

"I get it, I get it. And it's none of your business. And if that's some sort of sexual invitation, forget it. I'm not interested. I don't get involved with other people in the business."

No matter what she claimed, her body couldn't help responding to his incredible appeal. He knew it—the gleam in his eye told her that.

"I think I could make you very interested. But unfortunately, I'm not free to do dis."

"Oh." She ignored her stab of disappointment.

"Like you, I save myself for the stage. I make love to my audience, and to them only. Especially for Valentine's. Tonight, they deserve extra special loving."

"Yes. Exactly. That's what I do too."

"Den why do you look so out of sorts, ma petite beignet? You sing every night, you make love to your audience, and yet you still look as though some good old-fashion gogo would clear the cobwebs right out, eh." He snapped his fingers. "Dat's it! I have the solution. You're doing it hafass."

"What?" She gasped indignantly.

"Hafass, as we Cajuns say. Means half-hearted. When you open your pretty mouth and start singing, I will know instantly if you've been singing hafass."

Singing hafass? That was it. The final straw.

"Take dis." He slapped a pitch pipe into her palm. She nearly threw it back at him; she had perfect pitch. Instead she stuffed it into her cleavage and turned to the band.

"C flat. Follow my lead."

And they did, seamlessly, flawlessly, as she launched into "Blue Collar Boogie." Except this was a version of the song she'd never heard before. She'd written it, worked out the chords, slaved over the words, but she'd never sung it like this. Her song about wage slaves acquired a sexual undertone, as if it were being narrated by a hooker instead of a temp. Her voice had a husky edge to it that her vocal coach would never have recognized. And the way she was moving, rolling her hips, stalking back and forth across the stage—she never did that. Until now.

The backup band was fantastic. No one would have guessed they'd never even heard the song before. And even though she hadn't written a part for a horn section, they improvised during the bridge, where Josh would normally have taken the spotlight. The singer stood at the edge of the stage, arms folded across his chest, legs spread apart, and every time she caught his eye, she felt driven further, deeper into the wild side of her song.

And the way it felt … God, it was incredible. A mad, fevered wildness swept through her, the crowd, and the band. Power rushed through her, an electric confidence that arced into the crowd, creating a frenzy on the dance floor. Their stomping and swirling set her on fire, and her voice amped up to a decibel level she hadn't known she possessed. It was as if they were all connected to her, as if invisible fibers snaked from her vocal chords into their nerve endings, and back again. It was better than sex, better than the best orgasm she'd ever had. The only thing missing … was Josh.

The strange thought barely registered, she was so out of her mind. Nothing else entered her mind either during the madness of the next few minutes … or was it hours … or days … who knew? All she knew was music and singing and dancing and sex, pure, raw sex swirling from her, around her, back and forth in an endless stream of joy.

And then, suddenly, there was Josh. He was right in front of her, as adorable as ever, a sweet treat she'd denied herself for too long. She leaped on him and kissed him with everything she had. He staggered, then caught his balance and wrapped his arms around her. They kissed, deliciously, endlessly. The taste of him cruised through her bloodstream like an injection of liquid sunshine.

"Josh, I've been an idiot," she whispered against his mouth.

"Does this mean we can go out, since I've been a fool for you since day one?" He winked one hazel eye at her.

"Yeah."

"Does it mean we can finish the set?"

Startled, she glanced into the audience. The group was even smaller than when she'd left, but they were smiling. A few were toasting them with raised glasses of the hurricanes the bar claimed as a specialty. Who cared how big the crowd was, she suddenly thought. They were her crowd, they'd come to see Miss Jess, and she was going to sing her heart out for them.

"Absolutely. But you'll have to put me down."

"Only temporarily."

"Everything's temporary. Might as well enjoy it."

He gave her a startled look. She wasn't usually given to philosophical statements. She shrugged, just as surprised as he was.

There was no other way to put it; the rest of the set rocked. Rocked hard. And word spread throughout Frenchmen's Street, so by the time Arrietta was singing the last song, "Be my Honey Tonight," people were packed into Hurricane City, a few even craning their necks from outside. Arrietta was soaked with sweat. Even her hair hung in damp, limp waves, her careful marcelled hairdo long gone. But it was a good sweat, the kind you might work up in bed with an especially fine lover.

And she did that too. She and Josh spent the rest of Valentine's Night rolling around the king-size bed at the Frenchmen's Bed and Breakfast. All the pent-up lust they'd been holding back exploded into hours of hot, down-and-dirty lovemaking.

"Who would have guessed that a goofy bassist and an uptight singer would have such great sex?" Josh joked, after her third orgasm, accomplished by a demonstration of his skill with his tongue.

"I'm not surprised."

"Yeah? Then what took you so long to come around? I must have asked you out about fifty times."

"I don't know." She ran her hand down his chest. It wasn't spectacularly muscled, the way the Cajun singer's had been. But it was sturdy and firm-skinned, and she loved touching it more than she would have believed possible. "Maybe because I knew it would be this good. I didn't want to get into all that."

"All that?"

"This. Sex. Bed. Relationship. Love-type stuff. It's messy. Complicated." She said it dreamily, as if remembering something that no longer had any reality.

"It's not complicated from where I'm lying." Josh raised himself up on one elbow. "As far as I'm concerned, we're together, and the only one can change that is you. Because I'm not walking away now."

She smiled at his utter adorableness. "I think I might hold you to that." And she yanked him down on top of her for one more go-around.

The only thing that got them out of bed the next morning was checkout at eleven and the fact that they had to hit the road for their next gig in Austin, Texas. When they'd finally torn themselves away from the bed and dressed, Josh picked up a small silver object from the night stand table. "Pitch pipe? I've never seen you use one of those."

"It's not mine. It's from that singer, the one I went to yell at last night. I ended up singing with his band and I guess I walked off with his pitch pipe by mistake. Give it here. I'll drop it off at the bar before we go."

Josh gave her an odd look, but she was already packing her bag. "I'll swing by the bar and then meet you at the Café for breakfast. Tell Mackie D. too."

"Sounds good. I could really go for a few more beignets before we leave town."

The word beignet brought another smile to her face. Really, when she thought about it, she owed the Cajun guy a big thank you. Not only had she given two spectacular performances, but she'd finally given in to her feelings for Josh. Maybe she'd see him at Chez le Voodoo and could tell him so in person.

She dressed in a yellow sundress to match her cheerful mood and forged into the sunshine. Frenchman's Street didn't look nearly as dissolute as it ought to, considering everyone had spent the night partying. The brightly painted doors—cobalt blue, blood red—gave the street a quaint, ramshackle flair. There was Hurricane City, with a waiter sweeping the sidewalk outside. And there, right next door, Chez le Voodoo. She blinked. It looked a little different in the light of day. It still had that old-fashioned look, but now she could see that the gas lamps were fakes that held electric bulbs.

Inside, the place was empty. The manic energy from the night before had been replaced with a hung-over quality. Onstage, an older black man sat behind a drum set, tapping lightly on the cymbals. She approached him, armed with a smile.

"Good morning. I wonder if you could help me. I was in here last night and I got up on stage with the singer. Well, singer and sax player. I didn't catch his name, but he gave me his pitch pipe and I'd like to return it to him."

The man glanced at her indifferently. "Voodoo Ladies de only band here last night. All female in dat dere group."

She frowned. "That can't be right. It was an eight-piece band with a horn section. The singer was a tall, black-haired man with no vocal training whatsoever. They were singing 'Laissez les Bon Temps Rouler' when I came in. Much too loudly, I might add. The crowd loved it though. They were dancing up a storm. They were shaking the place so hard it felt like an earthquake."

The cymbals suddenly stilled, as he replaced his drumstick with his hand. "You saw Big Jack?"

"Big Jack? That's his name? That sounds right. Great, well, since you seem to know him, would you mind returning this to him? I'm sure he didn't mean to leave it with me, it looks like an antique or something."

"Antique." The man chuckled. "Dat dere item's 'bout a hundred years old, I'd say."

"A hundred. Wow. That's pretty cool. Even more

reason to return it to its rightful owner."

"Ain't no way to do that. He meant you to have it, sure 'nough." He shrank back from the pitch pipe. "I wouldn't touch anything from Big Jack."

"No way to do that? What do you mean? You don't know where he lives?"

"I can guess, right 'nough. It's either heaven or hell, and my first choice would be hell. Maybe I'll find out when I pass. Until den, I don't want nothin' to do with dat man. Stirs things up, he does. Always has, dead or alive."

"Excuse me?" None of that made any sense to Arrietta. "Do you know his last name? Maybe I can look him up in the Yellow Pages."

The man burst into raucous laughter. "Ain't no Yellow Pages where he's at. Just take your little souvenir and go, miss. Dat's my best advice to you. I'm surprised it don't smell like brimstone."

Brimstone? A chill went through Arrietta. "Are you saying..." She lowered her voice. "Are you saying Big Jack is dead?"

"Course he is. Ain't no man can survive a bullet to the belly. Fooled around one too many times, dat man did. Shot by a wronged woman on Valentine's Day, he was, right dere on dat stage. About a hundred people saw it happen. Some tried to help, but when your guts are spilled out, ain't much to do."

Arrietta stared, her throat gone tight and painful. All she could think was, that glorious, beautiful man...shot in the stomach. And now she remembered the weird shadow she'd seen on his belly.

"Don't look so burned, girl. Everyone said it was a good death. He died doing what he loved best, gettin' up on stage and singing his guts out. People say he's still singin', wherever he is, and wherever he is, dere's people dancin'. Some things not even de Grim Reaper can stop."

Arrietta shook her head, shaking off the strange spell of the man's words. "He can't be dead. He was here just last night. He gave me this." She thrust the pitch pipe forward, but again he shrank away from it.

"You the one with the visitation, girl, not me. Dat's your pipe. You take it and go now, hear?"

As if in a trance, she curled it into her hand, then blindly turned for the door. Just before she reached it, the man called after her.

"Next time you come to Frenchmen's Street, stop on by. If you're good enough for Big Jack, Chez le Voodoo'd be glad to have you sing a set or two. Open invitation, hear? You tell your manager."

"Thanks," she managed, before stumbling into the sunny street. Numbly, she opened her hand and looked at the pitch pipe. It looked ordinary enough, though of a high quality that spoke of the days before modern slipshod manufacturing. It didn't smell of brimstone or scorch her palm. Instead it had a heavy, comforting weight. Peering closer, she saw an inscription in copperplate lettering across the back. She had to squint to make it out.

Jacques Boudreau, May 14, 1890. Laissez le Bon Temps Rouler.

Okay then, Big Jack, she thought. Will do. From now on, the bon temps will be roulez-ing Chez Arrietta.

And she ran to find Josh, who was waiting with a sexy smile and a plate full of beignets.

No Beignet Left Behind *by Erin Nicholas*

"If you don't show up, I'm not returning your copy of Mama Mia or your dress and I'm taking your red Gucci shoes home to Houston with me."

Kara couldn't believe she was being stood up by the hot brunette she'd been looking forward to seeing for weeks. Ellen Bossard, her best friend from high school, laughed on the other end of the phone.

"I'll be there. Just later than I'd planned. I can't help the weather."

Kara wasn't sure she believed that. The Bossards had a lot of power. It wouldn't have surprised her if they could influence the weather. Plus there was the legend of their great-great-grandmother being some kind of magical Voodoo priestess or something. Ellen had always loved that piece of family history.

"I'm literally already in the cab, dressed, curled, the whole bit," Kara said.

"So, go. It's not a big deal. I'll see you there."

It was a big deal, though. She was going to crash Ellen's parents' anniversary party? No way.

"I'll just see you at the apartment," she told Ellen, feeling the crush of disappointment as she looked down at the emerald silk dress and glittering silver shoes. She *never* dressed like this unless she was with Ellen in New Orleans. But she did love it. Feeling like a princess for a night—there was nothing like it.

"I'm going to have to go straight to the party," Ellen said. "And you have to meet your ride by midnight, right?"

"Yeah." Kara slumped in her seat in the back of the cab. "This sucks."

"Just go to the party. I'll be there as soon as I can

and we'll have a little time before you have to leave."

Kara and Ellen were like sisters, but they hadn't seen each other in months. Kara had taken a job in Texas while Ellen's life had taken her overseas. Kara missed her friend and had arranged this trip specifically to coincide with Ellen's trip home for her parents' anniversary. But she couldn't afford to be away from work for too long, hence the ride-sharing with a friend of a friend's cousin to New Orleans and back in the span of forty-eight hours. The girl driving back wanted to leave by midnight so she could be home in time to shower and get to work.

Her ride, Brittney, was a friendly girl and they'd gotten along fine on the five and a half hour drive, but Kara didn't think for a minute that Brittney wouldn't leave her if she was late.

"I'm going to show up at your mom and dad's house without an invitation?" Kara asked. "I don't think so."

"They'll be thrilled," Ellen said. "They love you and haven't seen you in forever."

That might be true. She'd spent plenty of time with Ellen's family growing up. But Marianne and Raymond Bossard were intimidating people even over a casual family dinner—not that their definition of casual was quite the same as Kara's—and at a lavish masquerade party at their mansion with all of their friends and business acquaintances? Yeah, her palms were already sweating.

"I won't know anyone."

"Which makes the masquerade thing perfect," Ellen said.

Kara looked down at the mask in her lap.

She really did love the mask. She'd gone shopping as soon as she'd seen the gown Ellen had hanging in the closet of the apartment she used when she was in New

Orleans. She'd safety pinned a big K to it with a lip print in red lipstick in the corner.

Having a best friend with money always had and always would rock.

The Bossard mansion was one of the biggest in the Garden District. The Queen Anne style house always made Kara feel like she was stepping into a fairy tale. Ellen had grown up in the lap of luxury.

Kara had not.

But her grandparents had saved since the day she was born to send her to the exclusive private girls school where she met Ellen. They'd been best friends since the first day of kindergarten and through Ellen, Kara had experienced extravagant parties, exquisite gowns and shoes and accessories—the works. She had also learned poise and sophistication and manners. She could cover up her blue collar roots so convincingly that everyone who hired her interior decorating company, or who recommended her or who interviewed her or who invited her anywhere in Houston, assumed she came from big money. Big old Southern money.

Kara ran her finger along the glittery edge of the mask. She hadn't been to a good masquerade in a long time. And no one threw them like the Bossards. There would be a live band and real old-fashioned ballroom dancing and an unbelievable spread of food.

And, of course, the mask. A girl couldn't just wear a mask around every day, so it was hard to pass up an opportunity like this. The mask, like the gown, was a deep gorgeous green. It was trimmed in silver and had silver swirls looping around the eyes and across the nose, with a silk ribbon to hold it over her eyes.

Maybe she could do it. She'd been faking her background for so long that she had no reason to believe she couldn't do it with the Bossards' friends and colleagues. Maybe she could even make some business contacts.

"There will be beignets."

Four words. But they were *the* four words to get her into that party. Kara groaned. Ellen knew her too well. "You play dirty."

Ellen laughed. "You're just easy."

It was true. There weren't many things in the world that Kara couldn't resist. But the beignets that the Bossards' long-time cook, Gloria, made were number one on the list.

They were the beignets God would make if He got a craving. They were even better than the ones at Café Du Monde, *the* place for beignets in New Orleans. And Kara had eaten plenty of those in her life.

Kara's stomach growled. Eating prior to a Bossard party was a stupid thing to do. There was always an excessive spread of the best of everything, so she'd been fasting since breakfast.

The cab turned on to St. Charles Street and Kara resigned herself to going to the party alone. At least there would probably be an open bar. She liked hurricanes almost as much as she liked beignets.

"Fine, I'm here."

"Great. See you soon. Have fun!"

Ellen disconnected and Kara took a deep breath as the cab pulled to a stop. She wasn't actually worried about arriving at their party uninvited. But she was worried about tripping over her words...or the hem of her dress. For some reason, in front of the Bossards, she was a clumsy, klutzy mess.

As she got out of the cab and smoothed the front of her dress, she looked up at the mansion. The butterflies in her stomach kicked their swooping into high gear. Kara took a deep breath, then let it out through her lips in a little puff.   The cab pulled away, leaving her there at the end of the long, softly lit stone path that led to the front of the house.

And she could no longer ignore the real reason she was nervous.

Thomas was in there.

Thomas Bossard, Ellen's older brother. Ellen's very hot, successful, charming older brother who Kara had been in love with from afar since the first summer he'd come home from college.

Which would have been fine. If she hadn't *told* him she was in love with him the last time they'd seen one another.

Kara pressed her hand over her stomach where the butterflies seemed to multiply.

Of course Thomas would be here. But with Ellen by her side, he wouldn't dare bring up the last time they'd seen each other.

Ellen would definitely not approve of her brother spending time with Kara. Not because of Kara, but because Thomas was an infamous playboy. Ellen would want to protect her friend from his womanizing ways. But she had no idea that Kara was completely head over heels for Thomas.

When he'd e-mailed her that he would be in Houston for business and invited her to dinner, Kara had been unable to resist. He was an old friend, she reasoned. Of course she should see him if he was in town. She'd been in Houston with the interior design company for only a year and she was admittedly a bit homesick.

She'd hoped to eventually go home to New Orleans and open her own design company, but she knew she needed some experience and a chance to truly learn the business. So she planned to stay in Houston a little longer. Seeing someone from home was too tempting to pass up.

Especially when it was Thomas Bossard.

Thomas was tall—six-four—and broad through the shoulders, but trim. He kept in shape by running and playing racquetball. He had dark hair and deep brown eyes that always seemed to have a mischievous crinkle at the corners. He also had a killer smile. At least, the one he aimed at her had always made her heart threaten to stutter to a stop.

The guy oozed charm. He was intelligent and witty and polished and charming. He was exactly what her young heart had imagined a fairy-tale prince would be like and she ultimately compared all men to him. Not just the men she dated—though they definitely got measured next to the Thomas-Bossard-ruler—but also the men she encountered at work, the men her friends dated, and even her college professors.

No one had ever outshone Thomas.

But he was out of reach. He was from a whole other world, ran in a completely different circle. What did she have to offer to a man like that? A man who could have any woman in the world—and had, reportedly, had many of them during his travels.

He barely knew her name.

So when he'd e-mailed she'd been thrilled. And when he'd suggested going back to his hotel suite for a drink, she'd been amazed. And when he'd asked if he could kiss her, she'd nearly fallen at his feet. And when he'd asked her to spend the night, she'd... done it.

And after three earth-shaking orgasms, she told him she was in love with him.

And when she'd awakened in the morning before

he had, she'd snuck out.

Kara worked on breathing again. The breath in was good and deep and she let it out slowly, hoping to calm her heart and her stomach.

Making love with Thomas was the epitome of everything for her. And she'd snuck out quickly in the morning to avoid any awkward morning after routines or excuses or explanations. She didn't want a thing to mar the perfect memory—not even the delicacy of waking up in his arms.

And now she was standing on his front walk after not responding to any of his calls or texts. Or the five dozen roses he'd sent. Or the six dozen lilies he'd sent. Or the seven dozen rare tropical Crown flowers he'd sent.

Seven dozen rare flowers? Who did that?

A very rich man.

Okay, Kara amended, a very *romantic* rich man.

But still...each petal had just served to further illustrate how far apart their worlds really were. She'd never gotten roses. And she'd never dated a man who could afford two hundred and sixteen of them.

She was embarrassed that she'd thought for even a moment it could be anything more than sex between them.

Okay, she was either going in or not.

Ellen would be there soon. She'd be fine for an hour or so. She'd put her mask on, blend in, and find the beignets. How much trouble could she get into that way?

Thomas Bossard was bored. The kind of bored that even pretty girls in fancy dresses couldn't cure. He would have left a long time ago if it weren't his parents' anniversary.

He checked his phone. Maybe there would be a

business emergency. Unlikely since most, if not all, of the family's business contacts were here tonight, but he was hopeful for a diversion.

Or maybe his sister would have at least texted. It was also unlikely she'd need a ride from the airport—their limo was probably already waiting outside the terminal—but he could hope for a flat or something, couldn't he?

He strolled into the area off the main room where the food was on display and being served. He'd already sampled the prime rib, the jumbo shrimp, the asparagus spears, the breads, and the dozens of other dishes his mother had, predictably, gone overboard in adding. Now he was headed for the desserts.

But it wasn't the cheesecake or the crème brulee or even the beignets that got his immediate attention. It was the brunette in the emerald green gown and mask that he noticed first.

On first glance, she didn't seem that different from all the other beauties of the ball, but there was something about how curls were escaping her updo, and the streak of dust on the hem of the dress, and most especially the way she was wrapping a beignet in a paper napkin—and putting it in her purse—that made it impossible for him to look away. When she added a second beignet, he was intrigued. When her purse wouldn't zip completely shut over the contents, he was smitten.

Thomas propped a shoulder against the arched doorway and decided to watch. This was more entertaining than anything else going on so far. And he loved the curve of her neck. And the way she was smiling to herself as she pilfered beignets.

He hadn't looked at a woman as attractive or with any physical interest in two months. Seven weeks, four days and two hours to be exact. Not since he'd picked Kara

Jennings up in front of her apartment building in Houston for dinner.

He'd always found Kara to be beautiful and sweet, if a bit quiet—though next to his sister, everyone was quiet. He'd met her a handful of times, but hadn't paid much attention to his little sister's school friend. Until that summer he'd come home from Italy. Kara had been over for dinner with his family and he'd been struck speechless when she walked into the room.

She'd blossomed over the months since he'd last seen her. She had gone from beautiful to stunning and while she still seemed sweet, she'd also gained some confidence that made her speak up and share her opinion during conversation and even laugh out loud when something amused her. He'd found her completely enchanting and himself in a very unusual situation—he hadn't known what to do.

She was only nineteen, just finishing high school, while he was twenty-five and just moving into his new position as Vice President for his family's company. They were not only far apart in age, but also in completely different places in their lives.

He couldn't date her. He couldn't even flirt with her. He certainly couldn't take her to bed. All of those things would mean something very different to a young girl than it would to him.

And she was his sister's friend.

So, Thomas had squelched all his desires for Kara repeatedly over that summer when she seemed to spend more time at their house—and by their pool in her bikini—than she did anywhere else.

When she'd finally left for school in the fall, he hadn't seen her again.

Until she'd come home for Ellen's college

graduation. Again, the years had been more than kind. And when he'd finally decided to risk a conversation with her, he'd found her warm and intelligent and amusing.

He'd wanted her and had determined that, eventually, he would have her. She was the one.

When work at taken him to Houston a year after she'd moved there, Thomas didn't hesitate to contact her about getting together for dinner. He'd been thrilled, if not completely surprised, when she'd accepted.

And when she'd stepped out of the elevator in her building to meet him in the lobby, he'd been lost.

She was gorgeous, with the same sweet smile that always made his heart trip.

It was that smile that convinced him now that he knew exactly who he was watching stuff beignets in her purse.

Kara Jennings had come to his parents' party.

There was no way she was going to ignore him now.

Realizing she was not going to get her evening bag zipped, Kara muttered something under her breath, then reached to pull one corner off the top beignet to make it smaller. But Gloria's beignets were—as God intended them to be—covered with enough powdered sugar to choke a horse. A little cloud of sugar puffed up out of her purse then settled on the bodice of her dress. The dark green dress that showed every speck of white.

"For the love of Pete!" Kara exclaimed. She stuffed the corner of the beignet into her mouth, zipped the purse half way shut with a good yank, then turned.

Thomas assumed she was on her way to find the washroom. But she pulled up short at the sight of him in the doorway. She fumbled with her purse, then lifted her hand to her face before remembering the mask that hid her identity. Supposedly.

She chewed furiously, swallowed, wiped her lips with her finger and put on a charming smile. "Good evening," she greeted him calmly.

"Good evening." He gave her a half smile. "You're fond of the beignets."

Even with the mask in place he could see her cheeks get red.

"They're the best in New Orleans," she finally replied.

His smile grew. "You've had them before then?"

He could read in her eyes that she regretted the slip. Well, she wasn't going to regret anything else about this night if he had anything to say about it.

"I sampled them earlier," she lied coolly a moment later.

Why didn't she want him to recognize her? Because she'd been avoiding his calls and gifts for almost two months? Because she'd slipped from his bed before dawn, like she felt guilty or embarrassed about their night together? She was in love with him. She'd said so herself. This was ridiculous.

Thomas felt his eyebrows pull together and had to work to smooth his expression. He'd been stunned by the sense of loss he'd felt when he awakened alone. It was followed quickly by anger, then frustration when she completely ignored him. He'd been in Hong Kong for the past two months, preventing him from flying to Houston and camping on her doorstep until she talked to him. But even with the distance, he'd wanted her to know he was thinking of her and wanted to see her again when he was back in the States. In fact, he was quite afraid that she was the only woman he'd ever want to see again. He'd tried to be sweet and romantic. He'd sent flowers, cards, gifts. He'd called, e-mailed, and texted.

Well, if sweet and romantic wasn't going to work, then he could be direct and aggressive. He made his living being direct and aggressive.

She wanted him. There had been two of them there that night. He hadn't had the best sex of his entire life and fallen most of the way in love without some major participation on her part.

She wasn't getting away as easily tonight.

"Dance with me," he said simply, holding out his hand.

Her eyes widened. "Wh—what?"

"Dance. With me," he repeated. Once he touched her, once he had her in his arms again, he'd remind her of everything they'd shared. He wouldn't let go until she told him why she'd run.

She stared at him. "Dance?"

"Yes. You know how to waltz?"

She did. He knew she did. She'd learned in that very ballroom.

"Um, yes."

"Then, shall we?" He reached out and grasped her hand before she could answer.

"I—" She swallowed hard. "Yes. Alright."

"Very good." And it was. It was very good.

Thomas tugged her through the doorway, her beignet-filled purse bumping against his leg, another small cloud of white puffing from where the zipper hadn't closed completely. He stifled a grin.

"I got sugar on your pants," she said as he stepped onto the dance floor, turned and pulled her up against him.

"I don't mind," he told her huskily. He intended to

make love to her after covering her in powdered sugar later that night.

He lifted a finger and touched the corner of her mouth. Taking a smudge of sugar from her lips, he lifted his finger to his mouth and sucked it clean. And relished her quick intake of air.

Then they began to move. The music was as perfect as she was. She looked like she belonged here, like lavish parties and expensive gowns were everyday occurrences for her. But there was a wonder in her eyes as she looked around, a practiced feel to her dance steps that said they weren't quite as natural as she'd like, and every time her bag bumped against his back, he had to fight a smile. She was the only woman in the room with beignets in her handbag—of that he was certain.

They danced without speaking for two waltzes. Thomas just enjoyed the feel of her again, the smell of her hair, the way her hand fit in his.

Oh, yes, there was no way the sun was going to come up tomorrow without her in his bed.

"Let's go to the terrace," he finally said, dropping the dance pose and taking her hand.

She held back. "I shouldn't. I'm…waiting for someone."

He turned back with a frown he couldn't help. "A man?"

She looked startled at his fierce expression and tone. "N—No. Not a man."

"Who then?"

"Ellen," she replied. "Your sister."

Ah, his sister. Dammit. Ellen wouldn't like this. He hadn't told her how he felt about Kara, knowing that Ellen would assume her friend was simply another conquest. He hadn't had time to convince her that he'd changed. That he'd fallen in love.

"Then it's even more important that I speak with you now," he said. "Before she arrives."

Kara pulled her hand from his. "No, I can't. I'm sorry."

"Kara, I—"

Her mouth dropped open and she covered it with her hand quickly as she realized he knew her.

"No." She started shaking her head and backing away from him. "Oh, no."

He followed her, not caring that they were making a spectacle of themselves in front of all of his parents' friends and acquaintances. "Did you really think after our night together that I wouldn't recognize you simply because you wore a mask?" he asked. "That I wouldn't know the exact four shades of brown in your hair, that I wouldn't remember the freckle on your chin, that I would have forgotten the shape of your mouth after all of the things you did with it?"

Her mouth opened further and she made a little squeaking noise. But she kept retreating, backwards across the dance floor, with him in pursuit.

"You didn't realize that I'd lain awake stroking your hands with mine so that I know every inch."

Kara glanced down at her hands, then back to him.

"You don't know that I can close my eyes and recreate the scent of your skin, or that I can still feel how soft your hair is when I run my fingers through it, or that I can still recall exactly the sound of your sighs when I kiss your neck."

Her expression had gone from shocked to almost confused. And just a little bit... hopeful.

"You don't tell a man you love him and then sneak out of his bed in the morning, Kara," he said evenly.

She stopped backing up. She even opened her mouth as if to speak.

But just then Thomas' father pushed his way between them. His eyes were stormy as he faced Thomas. "Stop this right now. This isn't appropriate. This isn't the time or place."

Thomas started to reply when over his father's shoulder he saw Kara turn, pick up her skirts and run toward the door. He moved to follow her, but his father stepped to block him and put a heavy hand on his shoulder. "Let her go. You...acted without thinking."

Thomas became aware that the room was silent. The music had stopped, the dancing had stopped and everyone stood staring. He found his mother at the edge of the crowd. She looked stunned.

Well, he was feeling a bit flummoxed himself.

"I'm in love with her," he told his father gruffly.

His father looked him directly in the eyes. "She's not just some girl."

"No." Thomas shook his head. "No, she's not."

Raymond just looked at him for another moment. Then his father gave him a single nod and moved to the side. But just as Thomas started for the doors again, Ellen swooped into the room from the back of the house.

"Hey, everyone." Her big smile dropped as she looked around the room. "What did I miss?"

She'd just missed her best friend running away from her brother.

Thomas ran toward her. "Where is Kara staying?" he asked in a rush.

Ellen's eyebrows rose, but she didn't ask any questions. "My place."

"For how long?"

"Just tonight. She's catching a ride back to Houston

115

at midnight."

Thomas glanced at his mother's prized grandfather clock. It was eleven forty-two.

Ellen gripped his sleeve as he started for the door. "She's..."

"Everything," Thomas told her.

Ellen looked surprised, then she gave him a huge smile. "Go get her."

Thomas ran, finally succeeding in reaching the door, and tore it open with a flourish. "Kara!"

But there was no one on the porch or the front walk. He looked from side to side, but there was no sight of an emerald dress. He started down the steps, and almost stepped on a tube of lipstick, two sticks of gum and an ink pen. Almost as if someone had dropped her purse and spilled some of the contents.

He grinned and scooped the items up, pocketing them as he continued down the steps.

At the bottom, his grin grew. Lying on the stones was a beignet surrounded by a circle of powdered sugar.

Kara had definitely come this way.

He headed for the front gate. Surely she hadn't been able to get a cab that quickly.

But there was no sign of her as he looked up and down the sidewalk.

"Come on!"

He turned to see his sister jogging toward him.

"Clarence hasn't even put the car away yet."

Sure enough, their limo driver was having a cigarette before storing the car.

Within minutes they were on their way to Ellen's apartment.

"We only have ten minutes," Thomas groaned.

If she got in that car headed back to Houston, he

would just have to keep following her. Whether it was when they stopped for gas, or a burger, or even if they didn't stop until Houston, he was going to tell Kara how he felt.

"It'll be okay," Ellen assured him.

Finally, they pulled up in front of the building. Thomas bolted from the car and headed down the short alley to the set of steps that led to Ellen's front door.

He started up the steps, two at a time, but stopped half way up. His heart was pounding, but he was still able to smile when he saw a hair clip, a quarter and a cough drop that had clearly fallen from Kara's bag when she'd dropped it *again.* Because right in the midst of everything was the second beignet.

Thomas scooped it up and ran up the final six steps. He banged on the door to Ellen's apartment. A few seconds later, the door swung open and Kara stood on the other side staring up at him.

"You followed me?"

She no longer wore the mask or the gown. She'd changed into jeans and a t-shirt. There was a small suitcase sitting to one side of the door.

"And I intend to keep following you," he said, stepping into the apartment and pushing the door shut behind him. "But I'd love it if you decided to stop running away."

"I just..."

"I know." He took a step forward.

She took a step back. "I'm not..."

"Yes, you are." He stepped forward again.

"You don't..."

She stepped back again, but came up against the wall.

"Oh, I most definitely do," he said gruffly, pressing

close.

She stopped and sighed. "I just really…"

"I know. Me too."

Her eyes widened. "Really?"

"Really."

She smiled then. "Oh, good."

"Stay?"

She sighed. "That sounds really nice."

"It will be very nice." He lifted the beignet. "You left this behind."

Kara looked at it, then smiled a small sexy smile. "I really do love powdered sugar."

Thomas felt his heart expand and knew that he was exactly where he was supposed to be, with the only woman he would ever love.

After they kissed for what seemed like a year and a half, Thomas reached for the snap on her jeans.

"I should probably tell you that I happen to have a powdered sugar fantasy."

Kara began unbuttoning his shirt and pulling his tie loose. "Really? Tell me more."

"I intend to *show* you more. Does Ellen have any in the house?" he asked, unbuckling his belt and toeing off his shoes.

"Yes. But sadly no beignets to put it on." She gave him a wink.

That wink made him groan. "Prepare yourself. This could get really sticky."

Kara wrapped her arms around his neck and pulled him close to whisper against his lips, "But sweet. Very, very sweet."

No Last Calls *by Kinsey Holley*

"Am I *what*?"

"Honey, we want to help you, but you—"

Lindsey took a deep breath before answering. Lately, she'd been taking so many deep breaths before answering her mother that she was becoming permanently light headed. And if she kept gritting her teeth like this, she'd need caps.

"Mom, I'm not on drugs. I haven't developed a drinking problem. I'm not having a nervous breakdown." *Yet. No thanks to you.* "You need to stop this, okay? Just stop. Stop worrying, stop calling me a dozen times a week, and please, please, *please* don't talk to Ryan. He won't stop calling me! He's using you to keep a connection with me, and as long as you're talking to him, he'll think there's a chance we'll get back together."

"Well, of course there is! I mean, you can't ever say never, and—"

"Yes. Yes, I can. I already have. Never. I'm never marrying Ryan. See? I said it."

"Now you're just being childish," her mother snapped. Then, adopting the Very Calm Tone that always made Lindsey want to scream with frustration, she continued, "Why don't you come home for a visit. We can sit down and talk this all out."

"Mom. *Mom.* We've been over this a million times. I'm not gonna talk about this anymore. Nothing's wrong, Mom. I'm an adult. I'm doing fine. It's got *nothing to do with you*."

She glanced at the clock on the microwave. She was meeting Undrea for drinks. If she didn't leave right now, she'd be late and Undrea would be sitting in a bar by herself. Undrea knew the guy who owned it, but still. She was an old friend and the only one she really had in this city, so far. Lindsey didn't want to take advantage of that.

Besides, she was unfashionably punctual by nature. Her mother's influence, no doubt.

With another deep breath she said, "Why don't you give Dr. Kapinsky a call? Talk to him about how you're feeling. Maybe he can give you something to—"

"I do not need pills! This is not about how I'm feeling, it's about how you're ruining your life! I'll talk to you later, when you've calmed down and can discuss this rationally."

Her mother had been waiting almost two months for Lindsey to be rational. That was a problem, because in Cecily Holland's parlance, "rational" meant "agrees with me."

The line went dead, as Lindsey had hoped. She'd mentioned Dr. Kapinsky because she knew it would make her mother hang up.

Grabbing her purse, she locked the door and hurried downstairs. On the way, she did something she'd never done before in her life: She blocked her parents' home phone number and then, for good measure, both cell phones. *Just for a while, so I can get some peace.*

She tried to feel guilty about it, and found that she couldn't.

That had to be a good sign.

It was fortunate she'd been dressed and ready to go when her mother called, because it had taken her over an hour of dithering angst to figure out what to wear. Undrea had said she could go casual, wear jeans, but what did that *mean*? Was NYC "happy hour casual" the same as NOLA "happy hour casual"? Would she rather show up underdressed, or over? Jeans and t-shirt, or jeans and a flowy top, or jeans and something else?

At 7:30 in April, the temperature was still, and already, in the high seventies. She'd visited New Orleans several times, but she'd never been here in the summer. Lots of people had warned her it was worse than New York, which was plenty hot and humid in the summertime. On the other hand, one of the partners she'd worked for, a native of Mississippi, said he thought the punishing summers were a fair tradeoff for mild winters. He also said she'd find the French Quarter and New York resembled each other in two ways: they both stank like hell when it was hot, and you didn't need a car to get around.

In the six weeks she'd been here, she'd had no trouble making do with her feet, the streetcar and an occasional cab. She planned to buy a bicycle.

Her phone rang: a local number, one she didn't recognize. She hit Talk.

"Hello?"

"Lindsey?"

She halted midstep. A couple who'd been walking just a few steps behind bumped into her. Not bothering to offer an apology to the middle aged man and woman, who flashed her annoyed looks as they parted around her and continued together, she hissed into the phone, "Ryan? *Ryan?* Whose phone is this? And why are you calling me?"

He had the gall to sound wounded. "I'm here in New Orleans, at the W. I—"

"What the hell are you doing in New Orleans? Have you lost your mind? Did my moth—"

Another respect in which the Quarter resembled Manhattan: No one bothered to stare at the crazy lady screaming into her phone.

"I'm in town on business, honestly! You can call the

office and ask them! I haven't talked to your mom in weeks." She knew this was a lie, because her mother told her whenever she talked to Ryan. "Gerry was scheduled to take a depo down here but then something came up with Gresham, so he told me to—"

"Okay, okay, whatever. I don't care. Why are you calling me?"

"Lindsey!" Did he sound whiny, or was that just because she was so totally fed up with, over, and sick of him? Had he always whined like that? "I'm in town for a couple of days and I thought we could just have a drink, catch up. I mean, you won't talk to me when I call. I just want to see you, and—"

"No, Ryan. No. I don't want to, and there's no point. I'm meeting Undrea for drinks tonight and I'm busy the rest of the week. Get back to work, and don't call me again."

She hit End while he was still talking.

Was she going to have to change her damned phone number? And if so, how would she keep her mother from telling Ryan?

Maybe she could keep her father from telling her mother? No, that wouldn't work.

She needed siblings, is what she needed. Someone to leech the compulsive attention away from *her*. Way too late for that. She should've started trying to peel her mother off years ago; this situation was partly of her own doing.

I will not start ranting about this to Undrea the minute I sit down. I will talk about interesting things, not the same crap I've been whining about for months.

She remembered the phone call with Undrea that morning.

"I just think I need time to be on my own, to—"

122

"How long ago did you break up with Ryan?"

"Six months, about."

"How long have you been in New Orleans?"

"Almost two months."

"And how many dates you been on?"

"Um. None."

"So. You've been single six months, in New Orleans for two, and you probably haven't even talked to a man who wasn't driving a cab or a streetcar or standing behind a cash register."

"But, I—"

"You're not working. You've got lots of time on your hands, plenty of time to think about things, be on your own, get to know yourself, whatever you wanna call it—you can do all that and STILL find man-meeting time, do you understand what I'm saying?"

Lindsey was laughing now. *"Yes. You're saying you're not gonna shut up about this until I go out and meet some men."*

"Thank you. And I'm not talking about finding a boyfriend. Just dating. Dating's a skill, sweetie. You got to practice. And you know…the same's pretty much true about sex."

"NO. I'm not thinking about that right now."

"All right, we'll table that for later. Meet me at Possedé, Chartres off Iberville, six o'clock. You can wear jeans if you want. Don't argue with me, and don't you dare stand me up."

At which point Gerald, Undrea's loving and long-suffering boyfriend, yelled for her to get off the phone and give that poor girl (meaning Lindsey) a fucking break.

Possedé occupied the ground floor of a beautiful old red brick building with lots of black wrought iron balconies and trellises, another lovely relic of nineteenth century architecture in a seventy-eight by thirteen block area full of them.

Her Aunt Lee had long ago explained to her that the quintessential French Quarter architecture was actually Spanish, from the period when all this area had been under the control of that country.

The doors of Possedé stood open, as did the doors of most bars in the Quarter. The first thing she noticed when she walked in was that her black and white peasant blouse, blue jeans, wedge sandals and chunky silver jewelry constituted completely appropriate attire. The second was that the place was larger than she'd expected.

Beat up old sofas and coffee tables filled the area in front of the picture window facing the street. In the back corner was a dart board and jukebox, with a few more tables and sofas. The space in between was filled with tables. No TV sets, no sports memorabilia, just neon beer signs and Louisiana-themed posters. It had a retro vibe and wouldn't have been out of place in downtown Manhattan.

It was fairly crowded. Once she'd determined that Undrea wasn't there yet, she found a seat at the bar and waited for one of the three bartenders to notice her.

The guy on her left smiled at her and turned back to the woman on his other side, which suited Lindsey. It had been a few years since she'd done the bar scene as a single woman, and she didn't trust her chatting-up-strange-men skills in their current condition. (Undrea was right. She needed practice.)

When she'd caught the eye of a bartender, she ordered a Chardonnay. Then she pulled out her phone to check her email and maybe read something while waiting for Undrea to show up.

"Here you go, darlin'. Six dollars. You gonna pay cash, or can I start you a tab?"

She glanced up from her phone to see an entirely different, and much cuter, bartender than the one who'd taken her order.

"Um, cash please."

She fumbled for the money in her wallet as he waited for her, smiling.

"Here you go." She handed him a five and three ones.

"Thank you, ma'am." He pulled the five and one of the ones from her hand, then gently squeezed her fingers into her palm to indicate that he wasn't taking the remaining bills.

"No need to tip me," he said with a grin as he turned to the cash register.

It was a fairly spectacular grin. Wide and easy, like he was used to wearing it a lot.

"Okay..." she said under her breath.

Southerners were different from people up north. Still, she didn't know of any bartenders, anywhere, who turned down tips.

"So," said the Much Cuter Bartender as he turned back around, "you on your own tonight or are you waitin' for someone?"

"Waiting for someone."

"Male or female?"

She gave a little laugh, surprised that he'd stand here talking to her while the other two bartenders seemed to be rushing around like crazy.

"Female. I'm meeting a girlfriend."

"What's her name?"

"Undrea."

"Oh, yeah!" He grinned again. "So you the friend

she was telling me about? You just moved down here from New York City?"

"Yes. She told you about me?"

"Yep. She and Gerald haven't come in much lately, but I consider them regulars. Like 'em both a lot."

"Ethan!" one of the other bartenders called from several feet away.

Much Cuter Bartender—Ethan—held up a hand to her. "What is it?" he called back.

"Vodka martini, dry and dirty, Heineken draft, two Dos Equis and a glass of merlot!" The bartender sounded maybe just a touch hysterical.

Ethan rolled his eyes. "'Scuse me for a minute, darlin'. I'll be right back."

Was he flirting with her, or just being polite? It wasn't easy to tell with Southern guys. People down here regularly addressed strangers, as well as each other, with endearments like "honey" and "baby." And some Southern guys could call you "darlin'" without sounding like total douchebags.

Ethan was clearly a pro, his movements smooth and economical as he poured the liquor, filled the draft glasses, popped the caps off the beer bottles, and handed out the drinks to the people who'd ordered them. In marked contrast to his fellow barmen, he didn't seem rushed or stressed.

Afraid that he'd glance over and notice her staring at him, she returned her attention to her phone, relieved to have no new emails.

Suddenly she felt a pressure against her back. She turned around to see a guy in an expensive-looking suit directly behind her.

"Oh, sorry," the guy said. "I didn't mean to fall on you like that. I was trying to get to the bar, and...is it okay if—" He indicated that he wanted to put his arm in between her and the guy next to her.

She knew, she just *knew*—she always knew—that he was a lawyer. And cute, but nowhere near as hot as Ethan the Hot Bartender. And she was, she'd just that minute decided, on a lawyer hiatus.

But she'd let the guy get his drinks, so she leaned aside.

EtHB reappeared in front of her.

"Can I help you, sir?" he asked with a polite, professional smile. (And not the easy, infectious grin he'd favored her with several times already.)

"Oh, uh—yeah. Three Heinekens and an Abita. Thanks."

With his four beers dangling from between his fingers, the guy in the suit said to Lindsey, "You're welcome to join us, my buddies and me, we—"

"So," said EtHB, propping his elbows on the bar and looking straight at her. He was ignoring Presumed Lawyer Guy in a rather stunningly brazen manner, like he didn't give a shit if the guy ever came back or not, "when did you move to N'Awlins?"

"Um...about six weeks ago, maybe seven."

PLG stood there like an idiot for a couple beats, then turned and walked away.

The penny dropped. "You own this place, right?"

"Yep, I do. And how do you know Undrea?"

He wasn't looming, he wasn't invading her personal space, he was just focusing all his attention on *her.* That's what caught her off guard. He wasn't looking around at the other customers, or at his employees, or over her shoulder at other people in the bar. His entire attention was focused on her, and it was disconcerting.

Wait. Was it her turn to talk? Yes. Yes it was.

"I've known Undrea a while. She used to work at the same firm I did. I was in Manhattan and she was here in New Orleans."

"Right. One of the big ones. Winston, Winstead..."

"Winthrop, White and Strom."

"Right. I remember after Katrina, Undrea said they wanted her to move to Baton Rouge and she didn't want to."

"Well, she moved there at the beginning, when she thought they were just going until it was safe to come back. But then the firm decided to move there permanently, and she was already burned out with the huge law firm thing. So she came back here, to Delacroix, Mayes. She really likes it, too. She has time for a life now and everything."

"And you? You're still at Winthrop White whatever?"

The way he said it, it came out "whateva." She liked the slow, lazy drawl that so many people in the north thought irritating or, even more absurdly, indicative of a lack of intelligence.

"No. I quit a couple months ago. When I moved down here."

"Ethan!" one of the bartenders yelled.

"Hang on. I gotta go see what those dumbasses are doing now. *Fuck hell!*" he called down the bar as he walked away. "Are y'all new here or *what?*"

She smiled as Ethan yelled at his two employees. He didn't sound completely serious, and he was seriously cute. She liked tall guys. He was long and lean, with muscles, but not too many.

Naturally she'd just spent the past three years of her life with a guy who expended many of his scant off-hours at the gym. Ryan was proud and fond of his pecs and

128

biceps; he was in good shape because he worked out all the time and ate very carefully, but he didn't exactly have an active lifestyle. Office, gym, a bar a couple times a month. That was it.

Ethan looked like he probably did a lot of physical labor.

The first two buttons of his white button-down shirt were open. As he moved, she glimpsed the edges of a tattoo.

Ryan had a tattoo on his butt. Which totally which didn't count.

Ethan picked that moment to change out a CO_2 tank beneath the beer taps. She enjoyed watching his biceps as they flexed and contracted. They weren't bulky, not muscle-magazine-cover size. Just firm and smooth and fun to look at. *He* was fun to look at.

Hello, libido. Where the hell have you been?

"Lindsey?"

"May I have another glass of Chardonnay?" she asked Ethan.

"Yes ma'am, right away." He went to pour her glass.

"Lindsey? Hey."

"Here you go, darlin'—are you gonna tell me your name?"

She flushed, and smiled, and tried to pretend her hand wasn't trembling a little as she reached for the fresh glass. "Lindsey. Lindsey Holland."

"Hello, Lindsey."

"Lindsey! Hello?"

She suddenly noticed that someone new was in the seat to her right, and he apparently wanted her attention. Wait. How did he know—

"*Ryan?* Seriously? How the *fuck* did you find me?"

Ryan, with his hand on her arm, looked so bewildered, so confused, so sad, that she just wanted to punch his face in.

How could a guy who scored a 176 on the LSAT *be* so fucking clueless? Because it was cluelessness, not malice, that was urging Ryan on in his impossible quest. Of that, she was certain.

She didn't know herself all that well. But she knew Ryan, through and through.

"Your cell phone, Lindsey. You've got your location feature turned on."

Okay. Maybe she didn't really know him after all.

It took her a minute to find her voice, although she was shaking his hand off her arm before she even realized it. "I'm gonna ask you again—have you lost your fucking mind? How many times do I have to tell you I don't want to talk to you anymore?"

"But we *haven't* talked, Lindsey! We don't have closure!"

"*You* don't have closure, Ryan. I do. We broke up six months ago. I told you how I felt. We talked. That's it. That's all."

"But your mother says—"

"*Ryan!* What my mom says doesn't have a goddamned thing to do—"

"Buddy, you need to leave."

Oh, yeah. Ethan the Hot Bartender was still there, apparently now ignoring his two bartenders, and the customers at the bar, and staring at her and Ryan.

"I'm sorry," she said, flustered. "This won't—"

"Lindsey, why the *fuck* are you apologizing? You told the guy you didn't want to talk to him. And now he needs to leave."

He looked straight at Ryan. "Leave my bar. Now."

130

She glanced around, saw no obvious security guys.

"Wait a minute," Ryan said, going into I'm a Lawyer Mode. "I haven't done anything wrong, and I've paid for my drink. I just want to talk to my girlfriend."

"Ex-girlfriend," Lindsey snapped.

Ethan crossed his arms and moved back a few steps to lean against the back bar. "Ex-girlfriend means leave. Not gonna say it again."

And, she noted, the other two bartenders paused mid-service.

Ryan sensed that something had changed. "I don't have to go anywhere. I can drink here if I want to."

"No. You can't." Ethan gave her an enigmatic look, something involving a raised eyebrow, then yelled, "*Bottles down. Step back!*"

"Oh, fuck," someone near her muttered.

"Wait a minute! Whash goin' on?" someone else shouted. "Where's my drink?"

A waitress behind her sighed and replied, "Some asshole won't leave like he was told to. Now nobody gets served 'til he's gone."

That could be effective. Indeed, the crowd was starting to murmur.

"Hey, asshole," someone shouted. "It's the fucking French Quarter. Go drink someplace else."

Ethan the Hot Bartender was smirking. It looked good on him.

Ryan looked...queasy. Staring at her like she was going to save him.

"Ryan," she whispered, "leave. Just *leave.*"

He stared at her, then looked around the bar. People were muttering and cursing and—*whoa*. They'd even turned the jukebox off. Was this going to get ugly?

Ethan didn't seem concerned, though. He was just

standing there with his arms crossed, a tattoo on his upper left arm peeking out from his rolled up sleeves.

Where else did he have tattoos?

"I'm leaving. But I'm calling you again."

"Fine. I'm changing my number."

He looked like he was going to say something else. His faced worked, like he was trying to come up with the words, then he...just got up and left. As a bar full of people jeered and whistled and yelled filthy obscenities at his retreating back.

Just as they would've in a New York bar. She found this comforting.

"Okay, then!" Ethan shouted. "It's back on!"

Lots of whooping and hollering, but she could feel the tension in the bar starting to ebb. Happy hour was waning, and people were drifting out.

At that moment, her phone chirped: *"Whoo hoo! You have a text message! Yay!"*

It fucking figured.

Ethan seemed to know something was wrong. "What's the matter?"

"It's from Undrea." Sighing, she read the message out loud. "Client emergency. Prob here all nite. Call you 2morrow. Don't H8 me."

Ethan rolled his eyes. "Lawyers." Suddenly he straightened, tucked his shirt in, and said, "Come on. Let's go."

"Huh? Where?"

"I don't care. Let's walk around. Outside. Not here. These dumbasses are getting on my nerves, anyway. Rick!" he yelled. "I'm goin' out for a while. Be back at two!"

Rick, the guy who'd originally taken her order, didn't look quite so panicked any longer. He glanced at Lindsey and then nodded at Ethan. "Sure thing, boss."

"Lemme go wash up. I'll be right back."

Then he was gone, and she was sitting there, wondering what to do with the remains of her wine. She wasn't much of a chugger, and she hadn't had anything to eat since—

"Where's your go cup?"

She jumped, startled, to find Ethan standing behind her now.

"Huh?"

"You've been in New Orleans before, haven't you? You know you can leave a bar with a drink?"

"Oh! Right! Yeah, I forgot! You can walk on the street with a drink, and bars don't close!"

"That's right, baby—Vegas and the Big Easy. No such thing as last call. Or public intoxication, unless you do something really fucking stupid."

Ethan reached across her—she caught a whiff of cologne and sweat, and she liked both—to pluck a plastic cup from the bar. He proceeded to pour the rest of her wine into it.

"Ready?"

"For *what*?" she replied, kind of dazed by all that had just transpired in so short a time.

He grasped her hand in his—it was a strong hand, and a big one, and apparently he didn't think twice about grabbing strange women's hands, which she would've found kind of icky if he weren't so lean and hard and handsome and completely non-lawyerly—and then he was pulling her through the dwindling crowd and out to the street.

"Okay. You care where we go?" He stared down at her, his grasp on her hand not loosening.

"You do this all the time?" she squeaked, now finally, totally, freaked out by his easy, breezy, confident manner.

"Actually, no," he replied, cocking his head and giving her a searching look. "But I've had a crap week, and Undrea's talked about you a lot. And your ex seemed like an asshole and you're *very* hot. So I figure—let's walk around a little bit."

"Um, all right. Let's walk. And no, I don't really care where we go. I've got the Quarter pretty much memorized but I don't have any favorite places or anything yet."

They started walking up Iberville.

"You want to go down Bourbon?" he asked.

"Um...no. No, not really."

"Good—me neither. I don't think I've been into a Bourbon Street bar in a couple of years. Let's go down Royal instead."

"Cool! I love the stores down there. I got a really cool dress in that Voodoo shop a couple weeks ago."

"Gris Gris?"

"Yeah! That's the one."

The temperature had dropped a little; there was a nice breeze blowing. As they turned onto Royal, foot traffic got a little denser—lots of people strolling and looking in windows, as they were—but it wasn't nearly as crowded as it would be tomorrow night or Saturday.

They walked in silence for a bit, and it wasn't uncomfortable at all.

Then Ethan said, "So your name is Lindsey and you're a lawyer. And your ex is an asshole. Is he stalking you?"

She had to consider it for a minute. "I don't know. He's having a really, really hard time letting go. And my mom, she's encouraging him."

"So *you* broke up with *him*?"

"Yeah. And she didn't want me to."

"How long were y'all together? And why'd you break up? Unless that's too personal."

"No, it's not. We dated for three years. He asked me to move in about a year ago. And I said I would, but then I didn't. And then I said I needed to think about it. And then I realized that if I moved in with him, I'd end up marrying him whether I wanted to or not, and I knew I didn't want to, and I had to get out."

"You'd have to marry him? Who'd force you?"

She shook her head, embarrassed to be admitting all this aloud to anyone but Undrea.

"Nobody would force me. But, you see, I met him at Winthrop, White. And I worked a lot—a *lot.* Like, eighty, ninety hours a week."

He nodded. "Yep, that's Big Law for you."

She was struck by his use of the term. "You know people at big firms?"

"My dad's a partner at Lovell, LeVaux."

"*Ah.* Mine was a partner at Dyson Williams Jones. "

"Whoa. That's impressive."

"He just retired."

"So y'all met at the firm and started dating and you were so busy working that you never really had a life, so it took you a while to figure out Ryan wasn't the guy for you."

That stopped her in her tracks. He turned to look at her.

"What?"

"I'm a cliché."

"Huh?"

"I'm a fucking cliché! I never realized it 'til I heard you say it."

"I didn't say you were—"

"I'm twenty-eight years old. I went from high

school to college to law school to five years working eighty hours a week at a big firm. A couple vacations here and there, not many. I missed weddings, and birthdays, and funerals and, and life, you know? And now I'm burned out. Before I'm thirty."

"Darlin', lots of people have been through exactly what you've just been through, and—"

"I know! *That's what makes me a fucking cliché!*"

For some stupid reason she tried to pull her hand from his, but he wouldn't let go. He cocked his head (he looked so *sexy* when he did that) and grinned. "You know how I said you were hot?"

"Yeah."

"Well, you are, but you're pretty fucking cute, too. And you need to relax a little. Oh look, your wine's all gone. Come on."

He took the go cup from her hand, tossed it in a trash can, and started pulling her down the street again.

"Where are we going?"

"Don't sulk. Ladies don't sulk."

She burst out laughing. "Who says?"

"My mama. It's a Southern lady thing."

"I'm not a Southern—"

"Hush now. We're 'bout to pass a place belongs to a friend of mine."

They were on Toulouse now, walking south toward the river. The bells of the Cathedral rang the quarter hour. She glanced at her watch; it was already ten fifteen?

"Don't do that."

"Don't do what?"

"Don't look at your watch. You're in the Quarter. There's no time here."

She loved that drawl. *You're in the Quarta. There's no time hea.*

136

"But I live in the Quarter. How can I always ignore—"

"Here we are."

They were on the sidewalk in front of a place called Freddy's. She started to giggle.

"What is it?"

"Freddy's. Most names in the Quarter are like, I don't know—French, or sexy, or sleazy or something, you know? Freddy's could be a tavern in Brooklyn."

"It's not too creative, but the drinks are cold and the food's good. Hey, Francie," he addressed the girl who was manning the street bar, "I'll take a Corona. Think Derrick would mind if we got a drink from you but sat out here for a few minutes? It don't look all that busy in there."

"Nah. I don't think so. Here you go." She popped the cap off the beer bottle and handed it to him. "What about you, baby?"

Lindsey was still reading the hand-lettered list of drinks on the chalkboard. "I've been in New Orleans lots of times but I've never had a hurricane."

"Don't start right now. Trust me."

"Hey!" Francie protested. "We got some of the best hurricanes in N'Awlins! Better than Pat O's!"

"I'm not trashin' your hurricanes, woman! But my girl here's already had two glasses of white wine."

His girl?

Francie was making a face. "Oh no, baby. No. You don't need rum on top of that. Stick with wine or beer."

"Okay. I guess I'll just have another Chardonnay, thanks."

They sat down at one of the black wrought iron tables just outside the open doors of the restaurant.

"Oh God, that feels good."

At his raised eyebrows, she continued, "My feet. I've never worn these shoes before and I didn't plan on walking so much. I think I'm gonna kick 'em off for a while."

"Go right ahead."

She took a sip of her wine and sighed. It was better than the house wine at Possedé, but she didn't think that would be the right thing to say, so instead she asked, "Do you know everyone at every bar in the Quarter?"

He laughed. "Feels that way sometimes, but no. Fred's an old buddy of mine from high school. We flunked out of LSU together."

"Oh. Did you ever go back?"

He shrugged. "Nah. He did. I'm about thirty hours shy of a business degree at UNO but I keep getting distracted. The bars keep me busy."

"Bars?"

"Yeah. There's Possedé, and then my brother and me own a sports bar Uptown."

"Wow."

Her imagination was running away with her. In her mind, she was picking her parents up at the airport and driving them directly to a French Quarter bar owned by her tattooed, college dropout boyfriend with the accent thick as gumbo and a very casual relationship with proper English grammar.

"Whatcha thinking about?"

"Huh? Oh, nothing. So who's Derrick and why would he care if we sat out here?"

"He's the GM—the general manager—and it might piss off his wait staff if we sit down at a table without ordering anything from them. The street bar's for foot traffic, not sit down customers. But it's not busy right now and I figured we weren't staying long." He paused. "Unless your feet are hurtin' real bad, and then we could hang out and order some food. You need to eat?"

"I probably should. Let's get something—on me."

"No, ma'am." He shook his head and smiled. "It's on me. Hey! Shelley!" He motioned to a pretty blond waitress.

"Hey Ethan. What can I get for y'all?"

"You like raw oysters?" he asked Lindsey.

"Love 'em."

"That's it, then. Bring us two dozen." As Shelley walked away, he asked, "So. Where do you stay?"

"Excuse me?"

"Stay. Live. Where do you live?"

"Oh. I have a condo just a few blocks down from Possedé, at Chartes and St. Philip."

His eyes narrowed as he thought. "Oh, yeah. Yeah! That's a nice building. Really old. So...you said you're not working?" His eyes widened. "Oh shit, no. Forget I said that. That's just fucking rude, it's done of my business how—"

"It's okay! It's totally fine! No, I didn't buy it. My Aunt Lee left it to me a while ago."

"Holy shit. Nice aunt."

"Yeah, she was. She never had kids of her own, and we were really close."

"So you working? Or just taking it easy?"

She shrugged, not sure how to admit that she didn't have to work for a while. "Lee left me the apartment and some money. And I saved a lot while I was working, because I never took vacation and didn't really have time to spend it. So I'm just going to hang out for a while to decide what I want to do. I really *do* like practicing law. I just...I dunno. I guess I need to figure out the stuff most people figure out while they're still in college."

"Some people never figure that stuff out. You're actin' like twenty-eight is middle aged or something. It's not."

"How old are you?"

"Thirty. And bars and restaurants are the only place I've worked."

"How's your dad feel about that?"

"Well—for a long time? Not impressed. One of my sisters is a lawyer, the other is married to one. He kept thinking I was trying to find myself, or I needed some direction, or something like that. But now, with this economy? Law school graduates can't find jobs, but everybody still wants to drink. So, he's thinking I'm pretty smart right about now."

"You're originally from New Orleans? I mean, you sound like it."

"Yep. Born and bred. Dad's family's from Uptown, mom's is from Mandeville, which is—your aunt ever tell about Mandeville?"

"Yeah. Across the lake."

"Right. Nice place. Kind of sleepy, small, until after Katrina, when a bunch of people went over there and never came back. Hey! I could take you."

"Take me?" *Stop that, Lindsey.* Really wonderful nasty thoughts flitted through her head. "I mean, take me where?"

"To Mandeville. On my sailboat."

"You have a sailboat?"

"It's really nice."

"Oh....I'd like that. I love boats."

Ethan ordered another round of drinks, and she didn't protest because it wasn't like she was driving and besides, stumbling down the street was almost *de rigeur* for the Quarter.

"Where did you come up with the name for the bar?"

He looked a little embarrassed as he laughed. "My Cajun grandma—my mom's mom—gave me the nickname when I was a little bitty thing."

"It means 'possessed' in French, right?"

"Yeah. But in Cajun French it's a word for a...what you might call a troublesome youngster."

She laughed. "You're part Cajun?"

"Yeah. My great-great-grandmother was one of the most famous Creole courtesans in New Orleans back before the Civil War."

"Oh, that is so cool."

Their food arrived. "So, can Southern ladies slurp their oysters?"

"Hell yeah. So can hot drunk Yankee girls."

"Oh. You can tell I'm getting drunk?"

That damned *grin* again. "Don't worry, darlin'. It's cute on you. And I'm a total gentleman."

It was her turn to grin. "Yeah. I could tell that about you."

"My mama would be grateful to hear that."

It was hard—and gross—to talk while slurping oysters, so they ate in companionable silence. And she was thinking that this night had turned out pretty damn well, considering that Ryan had stalked her and Undrea had stood her up, and it looked like she'd made her second friend in New Orleans, and he was hot. And he thought *she* was hot. Which was hot. And the wine was cold, and the oysters were delicious, and Ethan was looking at something over her shoulder and he looked really pissed off...

He stood up abruptly. "Buddy, *you* are about to get your ass arrested. After you get it kicked, which is what I'm about to do."

Shelley came running up. "Whoa, whoa, whoa. Ethan, what's going on?"

"*Ryan???*"

There he was, standing right behind her, once again looking sad, and stubborn, and clueless and stupid and stalky...

"Lindsey, please. *Please.* I just want to talk. I don't want to—"

"Were you following me?"

"You didn't turn your location feature off, and—"

"Shelley, call 911," Ethan said flatly. "Now. This guy is fucking crazy, and he's a stalker."

And as soon as he said that, a cop walked up. A big, broad, African American street cop who looked like he could hold his own against NYC's finest was standing by their table with his hands on his hips, while passersby began to stop and stare.

"Ethan?" asked the cop. "What's going on here, man?"

She couldn't believe this. "You know all the cops, too?"

The cop looked at her. "Of course he knows all the cops. He owns a bar. Ethan, brother, what's going on."

"This guy"—Ethan stubbed a finger in Ryan's direction—"is following her. He's stalking her. She keeps telling him to get lost and he keeps showing up."

"I'm not stalking her," Ryan huffed. "I *know* her. I need to *talk* to her."

"No! No, you don't. I can't believe you're still doing this!"

"Ma'am, has he threatened you?"

"No. But I've told him, many many times, that I don't want to talk to him again."

"Okay, that's pretty clear. You need to move along, sir."

"But—"

"I said, move along, sir."

Ryan wasn't a short guy, nor a timid one—he was already an accomplished trial lawyer and it wasn't in his nature to quail. Unfortunately, like all good litigators, it was in his nature not to know when to shut up and go away.

"Wait just a damn minute. I know my rights. I'm a lawyer, and—"

"Oh, you did *not* just say that to me."

"What? Yes, I said I'm a lawyer! I'm with the firm of Winthrop, White and Strom, and—"

"Never heard of 'em."

"It's one of the biggest firms in New York City!" Ryan snapped.

"Oh, shit yeah," the cop smiled. "I get to arrest a New York City lawyer. Hang on there, buddy. I'm gonna call a blue and white."

"What? You can't arrest me!"

"Fuck I can't."

The cop was pulling his cell phone out.

This was getting ridiculous.

"Ryan! If you don't leave right now, I'm calling Gerry. And I'm going to tell him exactly what's been going on. And by the time I'm through, your partnership track will be seriously fucked."

Now he paying was paying attention. He looked terrified.

"Lindsey! I just—I just, I only—"

"NO. Leave. Now. Go back to the trial, go back to your life. Don't call me, don't call my mother. I have every text you sent me, Ryan. Every email, every voice mail."

143

Somehow, without admitting it to herself, she'd known he was getting weird. "I'll turn them over to Gerry. And he won't like them."

He looked ready to cry. And she had no sympathy for him. At all.

He turned on his heel and walked away.

"Well shit," sighed the cop. "I've never arrested a New York City lawyer before. And I've been working the Quarter over ten years."

"Sorry, Bernie. Maybe next time. But thanks."

Bernie and Ethan shook hands.

"Ma'am." He tipped his hat to her, then walked off.

She and Ethan were left standing, staring at each other. She took a deep breath.

"Look, I'm sorry for dragging you into this. I know he seems crazy, but I really don't think he'd hurt me. It's just, he's spent the last five years working as much I did, only he loves it. And he's a litigator. They really do think they're badasses, because they make a shitload of money and work for one of the world's top law firms. And a lot of women agree, so when I dumped him, he just couldn't...anyway. Sorry. He's not a threat, just a nuisance. And I *will* tell Gerry if he doesn't knock this crap off."

"Who's Gerry?"

"He's the senior partner Ryan's worked for since he joined the firm straight out of law school. Ryan's up for partner in two years, and if Gerry thinks he's gone off the deep end, or might do something to embarrass the firm, Ryan's toast. So I think he's gonna behave himself now."

"Huh. That's weird," Ethan mused.

"But it's totally normal in a big law firm, especially in New York. They're very image conscious."

"Huh? Oh, no, no, not that. I mean, my dad's firm wouldn't like it if an associate was harassing his ex-girlfriend. No, I just mean that, growing up, I *hated* the idea of going to law school so bad. My dad loves his job but he wasn't home much, and he was stressed out all the time, and I thought, I'm never doing that. So here I am, thirty years old, and you're the first lawyer I've ever dated."

She stopped short. "We're dating?"

"Oh." He looked briefly horrified, then sheepish. Lindsey realized it was the first time all night that he'd appeared anything other than completely confident. It just made him cuter, and it made her bolder.

Although, again, the wine didn't hurt.

"I'm totally fine if we're dating. But that means we have to, you know, go out on a date. Which means you have to call me. And you have to be patient with me, because I haven't been on a date in over three years and I'm not sure I remember how to do it."

This time it wasn't a grin. It was more of a leer, and she loved it. "I can help with that."

They were standing on the shared balcony of her condo, outside her front door. They'd put their numbers in each other's phones.

He was, as she'd suspected, a very, very, very good kisser.

"You have a really pretty throat."

"Aw, yeah. Hot Yankee Girl really *is* drunk."

"Okay, yeah, I am. So I'm not gonna ask you in, because I could get stupid, and—"

She absolutely *adored* it when a guy kissed her while she was talking. Or, at least, she had, until she'd started dating Ryan, who never did it.

Neither of them could speak while their tongues were entwined but eventually he broke off—with a delicious, tiny groan—and said, "Tomorrow."

"Tomorrow?"

"Yeah. I'm gonna sleep in."

"So am I. Cause I'm probably gonna have a hangover."

"That's okay. I'll be here round ten, and we're going to Café Du Monde for beignets and coffee. Best hangover cure ever. Then we'll see what happens."

She smiled against his lips. "I know what's gonna happen."

His arms tightened around her. "Yeah? So do I."

No One Drinks Alone *by Kelly Jamieson*

"Look at those hot chicks."

Kady Brandon turned and eyed the man who'd just said the words. Yup. He was looking right at her. He winked. She lifted an eyebrow and gave him an up and down look that made him grin.

Friday night on Bourbon Street in New Orleans meant crazy crowds— flirty men, people lining the balconies above them tossing shiny beads, loud pumping music from the bars that lined the street, and drinks to go. She and her two best friends sipped on hurricanes, sweet and fruity and laced with rum.

"I think those guys are following us," she said to Nikki and Megan.

The two girls laughed and shrugged. All three of them held the tiny straw of their drinks between thumb and fingers, and sucked back more of their hurricanes.

"Yeah, I noticed them before," Nikki said. "They're so cute."

"But this is a girls' night," Megan said. "Come on. Let's keep walking. I want to find that little Voodoo shop."

"Oh, me too!" Nikki said.

The three began to make their way slowly through the throngs of people. Kady snagged two more necklaces someone tossed from a balcony and draped them around her neck with the others, laughing as she did so. It was just so deliciously tacky and decadent.

Decadent. Yeah.

She paused to watch a man walk by wearing a full pirate costume. Whoa and damn. That was a fine pirate costume, with black boots, white pants and ruffled shirt, and a long red, black and gold jacket. The feather draping off his black hat bobbed as he walked by, and she turned to follow his progress, studying the costume. She'd always had a thing for pirates. Yum.

With a grin, she turned back to her friends, only to discover they'd disappeared. Shit.

She went onto her toes to try to spot them in the crowd, but it was impossible. The neon lights of the bars and shops cast a multi-colored glow into the dark, teeming street, disguising people with different hues and shadows.

"Hey, gorgeous. Drinking alone in New Orleans?"

Kady turned and saw the guy who'd been eyeing her earlier. His smile was wide and white, and faint lines whisked out from the corners of dark eyes. Just the right amount of beard stubble roughened a square jaw. Oh yeah, Nikki was right. He was cute.

"I'm not alone. I'm with friends."

"Uh-huh. You seem to have lost them."

She smiled. "Of course I haven't lost them. I'll find them."

"Of course." He lifted his plastic cup, which appeared to be filled with beer, and drank. "How about I keep you company while we find them?" He nodded at her drink. "No one drinks alone in New Orleans."

"No one drinks alone? Is that a thing?" Amusement curved her mouth as she pursed her lips around the straw of her fruity drink and sucked.

"Sure." His gaze dropped to her mouth and she felt a voluptuous kick of lust low down inside her. Heat rushed through her veins and her skin warmed beneath his gaze.

He wore a dark T-shirt over dark jeans. The T-shirt fit the toned muscles of his chest and shoulders spectacularly, and his low-rise jeans outlined lean hips and muscled thighs. His brown hair was a little long and flopped over his forehead in a sexy sweep that emphasized really nice eyes. But it was his smile that pulled her in, open, friendly, but with a promise of wicked fun. As if he knew exactly the kinds of things she liked.

"Come on," he said. "Let's walk a bit farther and see if we find them."

If he'd given off a creeper vibe, she never would have gone with him. But he didn't. He was sexy and handsome and nicely dressed, and when he set just his fingertips on the small of her back to guide her through the crowd, it was the perfect mix of direction and protection.

People milled around them, couples, groups, everyone talking, laughing, pointing up to the balconies where more people leaned with their drinks.

"They were looking for some Voodoo shop," she said, going on her toes to speak into his ear so she'd be heard over the music and loud shouts of enjoyment.

"There's one on the next corner. We can go check it out." He paused. "Hey, I'm Cam." He extended a hand.

She studied him. Okay. She could definitely do this. "Kady. Nice to meet you, Cam." She took his hand to shake it. His grip was warm and firm, his hand large and masculine.

"Likewise." His flirty smile and wink made her girl parts squeeze hard. Whoa.

He led her through the crowd, and with him at her side she had no fear of getting separated, the way he kept a gentle touch on her back or arm, and the way people moved aside because of his size and presence. They climbed the three stone steps into the small shop, the odor of patchouli incense surrounding them.

Inside the tiny store, it was easy to see that Nikki and Megan weren't there.

"Huh," she said. "I wonder where they went."

"This is a cool place," he said, picking up a small red pouch. He read the label. "'*A powerful magickal talisman for drawing love to you.*'"

Kady smirked. "Looking for love, are you?"

He met her eyes. "Maybe."

She shivered.

The young man behind the counter spoke up. "That's a very potent combination of ingredients," he said seriously. "Excellent for seduction."

More heat centered low in Kady's body and she pressed her lips together and glanced at the thin, sandy-haired kid.

"Gris Gris bags must always have an odd number of items," he continued. "The bag comes with an even number and you add your own personal item. You also get a bottle of love potion to dress the charm."

"What kind of personal item?" Cam asked.

The guy shrugged a narrow shoulder. "A hair, nail clipping, a photo."

Cam nodded and although his mouth was set in a solemn line, Kady hid a smile at the laughter lurking in his eyes. Then he reached into his pocket and pulled out a bunch of bills, peeling off a couple to pay for the Gris Gris.

"Give me one of your hairs," Cam said, once they were standing outside the shop.

"No way!"

Smiling, he moved closer to her, close enough that she could smell his aftershave, something clean and faintly citrusy. "Do you believe in magick?" he murmured.

She licked her bottom lip. *Maybe*. "No."

"Then give me a hair. What will it hurt?"

This was crazy. Voodoo magick and love potions.

Rolling her eyes, she tugged one hair from her scalp and handed it to him. He carefully put it into the bag and drew it closed, then tucked it into his back pocket. "There. Let's walk on," he suggested.

They paused again outside a club where two beautiful girls wearing tiny glittering bikinis tried to entice customers inside. "They're gorgeous," Kady murmured.

"Not as gorgeous as you."

"Oh, please." She rolled her eyes.

"Hey, you *are* gorgeous."

"Not like that." Those girls, probably exotic dancers, had perfect bodies, smooth skin and sexy glamour oozing out of every pore.

"Come on in," one girl called to them. "Ladies are welcome too."

Kady met Cam's twinkling eyes. "Let's go," he said with a jerk of his head.

"I can't go in there!" She laid a hand on her chest.

"Why not? You're with me. You're safe."

"I don't even know you!"

"Oh, come on. You know you're curious. I can tell."

She *was* curious about what went on in the "gentlemen's club," as it was called, still tingling inside from the erotic way Cam looked at her.

"We'll have one drink," Cam said, taking her hand. His grip felt protective rather than coercive, and curiosity and her adventurous streak won out. She followed him inside, letting the darkness and the thumping music swallow them up.

They were shown to two seats next to the stage where they ordered drinks from a scantily clad waitress. On stage, strobe lights flashed and one girl worked a pole with impressive muscle control, while on the right two girls moved to the music that Kady felt inside her like another heartbeat. Their sleek bodies gleamed, one with smooth chocolate-colored skin, the other creamy pale, their only attire a G-string. Kady found herself mesmerized by their grace and rhythm. Then the girls moved together and rubbed against each other.

Kady glanced at Cam, who also watched with rapt attention.

"You like to watch two girls together?" she asked in his ear.

He slanted her an amused glance. "What guy doesn't?"

She turned her attention back to the girls. The girl with long blonde hair touched the other girl's face and drew her fingertips down over her jaw, throat and chest. Kady's pussy clenched and she glanced again at Cam beside her.

Then the two dancers were holding each other's hips and rolling their bodies together in a sensuous slide, staring into each other's eyes.

"That's hot," Cam said.

Kady couldn't disagree. She licked her lips.

When the girls danced off the stage to approach patrons for lap dances, Kady's breath stuck in her throat. And then Cam held up a folded bill to get one dancer's attention. The blonde shimmied over with a shiny pink smile, shaking her hair down her back. She plucked the bill from his hand as Kady's eyes went wide. Was he really going to do it?

But Cam shook his head, eyes gleaming, a small smile tipping the corners of his mouth. "It's for her," he said, gesturing to Kady.

Kady's heart kicked against her ribs as she stared at the nearly naked woman only inches away from her.

The dancer's smile widened and she began to move in front of Kady, slow and sexy.

"You're crazy," she breathed to Cam but he sat

there in his chair, transfixed, watching with smoldering fascination.

The woman bent and cupped Kady's face with gentle hands, their faces close enough to kiss. Her smiling mouth hovered close, then she spun away and danced around the chair. Kady watched her hips move, envious of the dancer's smooth swaying. When she returned to face Kady, she straddled the chair and lowered herself to Kady's thighs, hips rolling in a back and forth movement that helplessly aroused Kady. Breathless, every nerve ending sensitized, Kady watched the dancer, her naked breasts almost in her face. Kady swallowed hard. Holy hotness. The woman's body rubbed against her, not really that close to Kady's pussy, but even so, it made her ache and pulse there.

And when she glanced at Cam, the way his face reflected her own flaming arousal made it even hotter. She was turning him on.

And then it was done. The music shifted into something faster and more aggressive and the dancers disappeared, to be replaced by others wearing tiny sequined bikinis.

"Okay, let's go," Kady said, a little dazed and breathless.

Outside in the warm, dark humidity, she sucked in a long breath. Her body pulsed with arousal and the lingering beat of the club music. She squeezed her thighs together against the ache there, then met Cam's knowing smile. Holy hell, he was sexy, with that grin that hinted of depravity and eyes that smoldered with lust. She couldn't believe he'd done that.

They made their way around a metal barricade at a cross street and paused on the corner. She took another breath and looked down the dark, narrow side street, old-fashioned street lamps gleaming off cobblestone sidewalks. "It's so pretty."

"Yeah. Come on, you look like you need another drink. There's a little place down here...it'll be quieter."

"And once again I'm letting a complete stranger lead me down a dark street."

"There are other people around. You're safe with me."

Sure. She was all kinds of crazy. But it was New Orleans! Bourbon Street! It was an adventure.

She followed him into another dark bar, this one tiny and cozy, with a small bar and a few stools and about eight tables. Instead of pulsing dance music, cool jazz drifted on the air. Cam continued right through the bar and pushed another door open, stepping out onto a small patio.

Kady gazed around. Candles in hurricane lamps flickered on wrought iron tables. Even in the dark, she could see the lush vines growing up the side of the old brick building and over a fence, with pots and baskets of flowers and ferns everywhere. The warm night closed around them again.

The wrought iron chairs scraped over old brick as Cam pulled a chair out for her and she sat, setting her small purse on the table. "This is lovely."

"Yeah. I like this place. Little change of pace."

"No kidding."

The waiter approached. "Another hurricane?" Cam asked her.

She shook her head. "I think I've had my fill of those. They're awfully sweet."

"Let's try Bourbon," he proposed. "Since we're on Bourbon Street."

"Well, technically we're not."

He grinned. "Smart ass."

They shared a smile as the waiter patiently waited for their order.

"What would you recommend?" Cam asked him.

"I'd recommend Maker's Mark. It's a softer whisky, subtle yet complex, with delicate vanilla and spice notes."

Kady met Cam's eyes and caught the gleam of fun there. "Sounds good."

The waiter nodded and disappeared back inside, leaving them alone on the patio.

"So Kady. What do you do for a living?"

"I'm a kindergarten teacher."

Cam coughed. "Really. And where're you from?"

"Alaska."

His eyebrows flew up into his long bangs. "Whoa. You've come quite a ways then."

She grinned. "I sure have. How about you?"

"I'm an accountant. From Fargo, North Dakota."

"Fargo!" She couldn't help but laugh. "Well, you've come pretty far too."

"I guess so."

Her body still buzzed with heat and arousal and when their eyes met, she shivered.

Their drinks arrived and they sipped them as they talked about eating beignets at Café du Monde and alligator boudin on Royal Street. More heat spread through Kady's body as she sipped her Bourbon. She probably should have ordered something colder. Something with ice. A *lot* of ice.

When their small glasses were empty, Cam reached for his wallet. Kady immediately picked up her purse.

"No, no." He waved a hand. "I'm buying."

"No one drinks alone," she murmured. "Doesn't mean you have to buy me drinks. And you bought the last round."

His smile made her pulse flutter.

"I'm buying," he said firmly. He left some bills on the table and once more guided her out to the street. "Where to now?"

Kady's cell phone buzzed in her purse. She pulled it out and peered at it. "It's a text from my friends," she said slowly. "Wanting to know where I am."

Their eyes met. He lifted one eyebrow. "Tell them you're fine," he murmured.

She studied his face, the humor and attraction gleaming in his eyes, the way he watched her with hot awareness. Tension hummed between them, the warm night air almost crackling with sexual exigency. She swiped her tongue over her bottom lip, and those eyes got even darker. "Okay."

Cam began to walk slowly along the sidewalk, leading Kady away from Bourbon Street as she thumbed a message into her phone. The noise of the huge block party faded away behind them as they approached a park. He watched her profile—her small nose, full lips, and long eyelashes that fluttered as she concentrated on her phone. A street lamp highlighted the curve of her cheek, a high cheekbone and smooth skin. Damn. She was just as gorgeous as any of those dancers—more so, in fact.

A kindergarten teacher. Getting a lap dance. A laugh bubbled up inside him and he swallowed it. The bourbon spread warmth through him, and his dick was still half hard. Watching those two dancers together had been hot, but watching Kady with the blonde had had his dick lengthening and thickening against his thigh, making him shift in his chair. Then watching Kady across that small table on the intimate little patio as she sipped her bourbon and talked and laughed had not helped his state of arousal. She was sexy as fuck.

They paused on the next corner, two quiet, narrow streets intersecting. Darkness shrouded them. Another couple passed by on the sidewalk opposite them, and farther up the street a few other people walked. Palm trees swayed and rustled in the soft night breeze, and the faint strains of a saxophone wafted up the street. She slipped her phone back into her purse and looked up at him. She wasn't tall—the top of her head came to his chin—but her legs were long in proportion to her body. The light wind ruffled her chin-length dark hair, and her lips shone. So pretty. Her body was pretty too, just the right amount of curve, with a small waist and full breasts. Like him, she wore a T-shirt and jeans, her shirt white, with little sleeves and a glittery silver logo that said "French Quarter". Red, gold, silver and green beads hung around her neck, and between the hem of the shirt and her low rise jeans, a peek of smooth golden skin tempted his hands to touch.

He set his hands on her hips.

"What are you doing?" she said, as they stood there on the dark corner facing each other.

He began to move. "Dancing."

She blinked. The saxophone was barely audible, wherever it was coming from. But then she smiled, a slow, sexy smile, and lifted her hands to his shoulders. Her touch felt good, her palms warm through his shirt, and she swept them over the cotton once, twice, a third time before settling her hands there. They moved together in a slow dance, eyes fastened on each other, their bodies drawing closer together until their hips touched and her breasts grazed his chest. Her thumbs brushed the skin of his neck just at the collar of his shirt, and his skin prickled all over.

God, she was sweet. His hands slid around her hips to cup her ass, bringing her up against him and her lips parted as she gazed up at him. And then he did what he'd wanted to all evening—he bent his head and kissed her.

Their mouths fit together perfectly, opening to each other, and he licked his way inside, tasting the spice and vanilla of the bourbon and the innate sweetness of her, pushing her lips farther apart with a ravenous hunger. She made a soft noise in her throat and her fingers slid over the nape of his neck and up into his hair, her nails scraping over his scalp. Sensation rolled over him, hot and urgent, his cock throbbing against her softness.

He sucked her tongue and she moaned again, tugging his hair.

Sharp need rocketed through him, heat spiraling fast and hot. His fingers dug into her ass and he wrapped his arms around her.

"God," she gasped when he lifted his mouth. "Oh my god."

"My hotel's close to here," he breathed.

"Oh yeah?"

"Yeah. The Château Orleans."

"That's a nice hotel." She gave him a sexy, assessing look up through her long eyelashes, fingers still playing in his hair. "I guess that means your accountant job pays well."

He grinned. "Or I'm a drug dealer."

A peal of laughter escaped her at that.

"So will you come back to my room with me?"

"I shouldn't be doing this," she murmured, petting his shoulder again. "Sex with a stranger...so dangerous..."

"You want to do it."

Her little tongue came out to drag over that plump bottom lip again, and his dick twitched.

"Yeah," she admitted. "I do."

"Then let's go."

This time he moved faster, taking big strides, and she hurried to keep up with him as they walked hand in hand. They entered the hotel lobby with its elegant columns and feathery potted palms in front of arched windows, crossed the black and white tile floor and climbed the wide staircase to the second floor.

"Your room is huge," she said as they entered. He'd left a lamp on beside the bed, illuminating the snowy white duvet cover on the king size bed.

"Big is always better. Right?"

She hopped onto the bed and smirked at him. "That sounds promising."

"Well, I don't like to brag." He sauntered toward her. "But my dick is so big it graduated from college a year ahead of me."

She dissolved into giggles, falling onto her back on the bed. "Oh. My. God."

He leaned over her, supporting himself with a hand on either side. "I hope I didn't just kill the mood."

She choked on another laugh. "You totally did. It might be hard to get it back."

"It's hard all right." He set his hands on her waist and lifted her up farther onto the bed. She kicked off her flip flops and he couldn't resist picking up one small foot, circling her bare ankle where her jeans were rolled up. He kissed the top of her foot. He wanted to drag his tongue over her body, tasting her everywhere. He slid his mouth to the inside of her ankle, opened it over the soft spot beneath her ankle bone and gently sucked.

He peered up at her face, where her eyes had gone hazy and her smile had softened.

"That's working," she said breathlessly.

He reached for the button of her jeans, lowered the zipper and then tugged them down over her hips and legs. He studied her smooth limbs and the tiny pink panties, so sheer he could see her patch of dark pubic curls. "Very pretty," he said, touching the little satin bow. He brushed his fingertips over her lower belly and she quivered.

"Thank you."

"Sex with a stranger, huh," he murmured. "You sure, gorgeous?"

She bit her lip. "I know it's wrong. But yeah, I'm sure. Um...you have something, right?"

One corner of his mouth lifted. "Seriously? You're going to make me use a condom?"

She gave him a long look.

He sighed.

"Don't be a jackass," she said.

He went into the bathroom and dug into his shaving kit, thankfully finding one small package at the bottom. While there, he sent a quick text to one of his buddies, which got an immediate reply. Back in the bedroom, he yanked his T-shirt over his head, then kicked off jeans, underwear and leather flip flops.

Her admiring gaze made his cock bob. Christ, he was so hard he hurt. He ran a hand down the length of it, balls tortuously tight. "You look hot like that," he rasped. "Lying there in that little T-shirt and panties and those beads. You know what that makes me wonder."

"What?"

"Did you show your tits to get the beads?"

She fluttered her eyelashes at him. "Keep wondering."

"Jesus."

"Should I take them off? Or leave them on?"

"Off. Definitely off."

As she sat up and removed the beads from around her neck then pulled off her T-shirt and bra, he rolled the condom onto his aching shaft then climbed onto the bed beside her. She pushed down the panties and dropped them over the side of the bed. He laid a hand on her stomach, then slowly slid it up until it rested between her breasts.

"Just as pretty as I thought," he whispered, studying the soft curves tipped with tight rosy nipples.

"Touch me," she begged softly. "Please."

"Touch you where?"

"Oh god. Everywhere."

"Your nipples?" He brushed his fingers over one taut peak.

She groaned. "Yes."

"Your pussy?" He slipped his hand down between her thighs. Moist heat met his palm and he held her there as he lowered his mouth to hers for another kiss. Long. Slow. Sweet.

Their tongues slid against each other, and her pussy pulsed into his palm. Her legs shifted restlessly. "Need you," she whispered, reaching for him. Her hands gripped his biceps and he flexed them. "Inside me."

"Just where I want to be."

He moved over her, kneeing her thighs apart, taking in the pink folds he revealed, so plump and delicate. He licked his lips, fever coursing through his veins, and leaned down to taste a beaded nipple. He pulled it softly, slowly into his mouth. Her body tightened and she sucked in a sharp breath. The sweet nub fit perfectly to his tongue and he sucked at it, tugging it, plumping her breast with his hand. Good Christ, she was gorgeous, perfect, amazing. He moved to the other nipple and did the same, until she writhed beneath him and he lifted up.

"I'm sorry," he growled. "This is gonna be fast. I'll make it up to you."

A sexy smile curved her lips as he went back onto his knees and fisted his cock. "I'll hold you to that."

"You can hold me to anything you want." He slicked the head of his cock through her creamy sex lips. "Preferably your sexy body. Christ, you're wet."

"I know. I'm aching for you. Do it. Do me. Please."

He pushed in, unable to wait another second, tension gathering at the base of his spine already.

He lifted her legs, pushing them up and back, opening her to him. His gaze moved between watching his gleaming cock slide in and out of her pussy and watching her face, the way her cheeks flushed, her lips trembled and her eyelashes fluttered over eyes glittering with need. Her bare breasts quivered with each push into her body, and her whimpers filled his ears. "Good?" he asked hoarsely.

"So good. God."

He rolled his hips, his cock surging into her and dragging out with sublime friction. They watched each other, a heated connection drawing out between them, unbearably intimate, unspeakably beautiful. His chest ached and he felt full, brimming with emotion. Jesus.

He fell over her, burying his face in the side of her neck, breathing in her scent, flowery and delicate and female. He fisted his hands in her hair as he rocked his body against hers, pumping into her again and again, driving hard and deep. His ass clenched, his thighs quivered and his skin buzzed. Pressure built, sensation gathered. Her pussy tightened around him and then rippled as she came with a long, low wail. Her hands gripped his back and he let himself go with one last drive into her sweet body, ecstasy exploding and blinding him, violent pleasure ripping through him in exquisite, erotic pain. He gasped and held himself inside her as he ejaculated in long, hard pulses.

"Fuck, Kady. Holy fucking hell."

She mumbled her agreement, hands moving on his sweat-dampened back.

They lay together for a long time, silent other than ragged breathing and the occasional soft sigh that escaped her lips. The ceiling fan above them cooled their overheated bodies.

Eventually, he moved off her and left the bed to get rid of the condom. When he returned she'd rolled to her side and watched him cross the room. He sat on the bed. "You're going to think this is really crazy," he murmured, brushing a strand of dark hair off her cheek. "But I think we should get married."

Her mouth fell open. "Married."

"Yeah. Tomorrow. Let's do it."

"That *is* crazy." Then she hopped up onto her knees and bounced on the mattress. "But it's the *best* idea!"

He laughed. "All right then."

"You do know in Louisiana there's a seventy-two hour waiting period between getting the marriage license and getting married."

"Yeah." He grinned. "So it's a good thing we got the license when we got here two days ago."

She laughed and crawled onto his lap, flinging her arms around his neck. "That's for sure. God, Cam, I can't wait to marry you tomorrow."

Their mouths met again in a hard, exuberant kiss.

"Where the heck is our wedding party?" she murmured. "Don't they even care that we disappeared?"

"Jim and Raj found Megan and Nikki. I texted Jim

and told him we're having pre-marital sex."

A laugh bubbled up her throat. "Cam!"

"What? It's not like they don't know we have sex. We've been living together for a year."

"But...they don't know about our...play acting stuff. Do they?"

"No. Our little fantasy role playing is just for us, don't worry." He kissed her nose. "Jesus, woman—I can't believe you made me wear a condom!"

She giggled and pushed at his shoulder. "It was part of the act."

"And a kindergarten teacher? From Alaska?"

"What? What's wrong with Alaska? I mean, *Fargo*? Come on! You did better last time, when you pretended to be an artist from New York who needed me to pose nude for his painting."

They kissed again.

"Mmm. That reminds me. I saw a pirate," she said against his lips. "On Bourbon Street. A sexy pirate."

"We could get you a sexy wench costume."

She licked her lips as heat flared low down inside her. "That would be fun."

"Married to you, things will never get boring," he murmured. "How did I ever get so lucky to find a girl like you?"

"You just don't want to drink alone."

He laughed and smooched her mouth again. "Well, there is that."

"But seriously, I know what you mean. It's finding someone who has that...something. That indefinable something that I thought was only inside me. But you have it too." She threaded her fingers through his hair. "You get me. You like to play and have adventures. I love you, Cam."

164

"Love you too, babe. So much. Marry me?"

"Yes, please. Right here in this hotel tomorrow."

Sax on a Stick *by Kate Davies*

He arrived before sound check.

The bar was almost empty, just a couple of old timers at the table near the window, nursing drinks that had long turned to melted-ice-water. The bartender nodded briefly at him as he made his way to a two-seat table along the far side of the dance floor. He sat, easing back into the wooden chair as he checked the angle. Yeah, even once the dancing started he'd have a perfect view of the stage.

Taking out his phone, he checked it for non-existent messages, figuring if he looked busy no one would pay attention to him sitting here well before the show was even scheduled to start.

It was a transparent and slightly pathetic effort, but worth a try.

The bartender crossed the dance floor, beer in hand. "Here you go, man," she said, her blond hair swinging as she set it on the table. "Your usual."

He smiled awkwardly up at her. Dammit. He couldn't decide if that was awesome customer service, or if he'd just been outed as the creeper who'd been stalking this band for the past several weeks.

Probably a little of both.

"Thanks," he finally said, digging into his back pocket for his wallet.

She waved him off. "I figure you're gonna be here for a while. Want to start a tab?"

Henodded. Sure, why not. It would definitely make things easier.

"What's your name?" She smiled at him. "So I can put it in the computer."

"James," he finally answered. "James Michel."

"Not Bond?" She teased. With a wink, she headed back to the bar. Over her shoulder, she added, "Let me know when you need another. It'll get pretty crowded in here soon."

Yeah, he knew. It was why he had been arriving at Dupre's earlier and earlier each week. It was the only way to make sure he had a good viewing spot.

And as lovely as the young lady was, he wasn't here to scope out the bartender.

No, he had his sights on someone else.

The thump-thump of an electric bass pulled his attention back to the stage, where one of the musicians was already warming up. Crap, was it that late already? He checked his watch. Still a little over an hour until the show started.

Well, the official show. For him, the show started...

He looked at the stage again. Another musician was pulling his instrument out of the case and fitting it together.

Yep. The show started right...about...now.

The Businessman was here again.

Breaux glanced at the small table out of the corner of his eye, pretending to focus on setting up his sax.

It was a good cover. He could put that beauty together with his eyes closed.

He didn't know the guy's name. He didn't know for certain that he was a businessman, for that matter.

But it seemed like a pretty reasonable guess. Button down shirt, sleeves rolled up partway in deference to the heat, khaki pants, nice watch that he was currently checking again.

One minute later than the last time you looked.

167

His sandy blond hair was cut short, barely brushing the tops of his ears. Breaux couldn't tell if his eyes were blue or brown—he'd never sat close enough for anyone to see from on stage—but even from this distance he could tell the guy had the longest damn eyelashes he'd ever seen.

When he'd first started showing up at their weekly gigs, Breaux had assumed he was there to meet women. God knew there were enough of them who came to the shows. But he never danced, never picked anyone up, just sat there nursing his beer and watching the band.

Watching Breaux.

Frankly, he was tired of it. And tonight he was going to do something about it.

James leaned back in his chair and crossed his arms over his chest. It was almost time for sound check.

Yeah, okay, it was a little pathetic that he knew the schedule so well, knew the steps the band would take to get ready for the night's performance before they even took them. Every week, without fail, he spent his Thursdays here. At first, he told himself it was for the music. That was all, just a chance to listen to some hot New Orleans style jazz performed by some of the best musicians in town. And in a town like NOLA, that was saying something.

He wasn't the only one who felt that way, either. Every week, the crowd got bigger, more enthusiastic. There'd been write ups in some of the local magazines and on entertainment websites, not that he'd set up a Google alert for the band's name or anything.

Oh, hell, yes he had.

He was a damn groupie.

Mentally rolling his eyes at himself, he lifted a hand

to signal the bartender. She nodded and went to get him another beer.

There really wasn't anything wrong with being a groupie, he supposed. He wasn't hurting anyone, just sitting here enjoying the show, building up some fantasy material for when he was home alone.

It wasn't like the sax player would ever notice him, anyway. He had his pick of women every week, hanging all over him, asking him to sign autographs and sometimes body parts. He'd never given any sign that he played for the other team.

And James wasn't the type to march on up to some hot guy and ask him out.

He was too reserved for that.

Plus, it was a handy way to get gay bashed, even in a cosmopolitan city like New Orleans.

So he'd just enjoy the hot music, the hotter guy playing it, and go home alone like every week.

Breaux ran a few scales on his alto, tossing in some arpeggios and a triplet or two. Starting soft and growing loud, then heading the other direction, he made that baby growl and moan as he worked through his warm up. Out of the corner of his eye he saw The Businessman shift in his chair, angling his body so he had a better view.

Yeah, he was watching.

Breaux smiled around his mouthpiece. If the man wanted to watch, he was damn well going to put on a show.

It was no secret that Breaux was a bit of an exhibitionist. All professional musicians had a touch of that in their personalities, at least the ones he knew. Getting up on stage night after night, all eyes on him, was a rush he never got tired of.

But when he had the opportunity to play to one face in the crowd, to feel that feedback loop of energy across the club...damn.

The set hadn't even started yet tonight and he was already on fire.

Leaning forward, he made that baby growl again.

"Jesus, Breaux, save some for the show," Junior muttered, nudging him with a hip as he tuned his guitar. "Not like there's anyone here to appreciate it yet."

Breaux lifted one hand from his sax, flipped off his bandmate, and went back to his warm ups.

This was just the appetizer. And he was getting amped up for the main dish.

God, the man was hot.

Sexy, dirty hot. His softly faded jeans were tight, clinging to every curve, and ripped in all the right places. He wore a black tank that already looked slightly damp from the musician's exertion. His shaved head gleamed under the stage lights. A trimmed goatee framed full lips currently wrapped around his saxophone mouthpiece.

God *damn,* James had it bad.

Sex On A Stick leaned over to say something to the keyboard player, pulling a full throated laugh out of the larger black man. "You're a dog, bro," he announced, smacking the saxophonist on the arm. "Grade A number one hound."

In response, the man threw his head back and howled. Straight up howled at the pressed-tin ceiling.

James shivered. He was going to have some sweet sound effects to go with his fantasies tonight.

The bar was really starting to fill up now, with locals and tourists in about equal proportions. A group of women all wearing fuchsia wigs and tight black t-shirts emblazoned with "Wedding Party" in sequins across their chests crowded around the bar. The woman in the middle, her shirt spelling out "I'm The Bride, Bitch", ordered hurricanes for all of them.

James smiled to himself. He'd tried those a few times, just because it was New Orleans and the drink was synonymous with the city, but found them too sweet for his taste. Give him a beer or a bourbon any day of the week.

Sex On A Stick ran some scales, notes so fast they tumbled over each other, and the waterfall of sound pulled James' attention away from the bachelorette party. He sat back in his chair, crossing one leg over the other, and settled in for yet another Thursday night of amazing music.

The bar was packed.

Breaux looked around at the gathered crowd and nodded with satisfaction. When they'd started this regular Thursday gig, attendance was pretty typical for midweek in New Orleans. But over the past few months, word had gotten around, and now they were bringing in enough customers to keep the owner happy.

Breaux and the rest of the band appreciated it, too. Not just for the increased revenue for the bar, and the job security that came from that. Not just for the added tips they collected every week. But the energy the crowd contributed made every week that much better. He fed off it, breathed it in, let it pump his performances up until he was flying high on the feedback loop from audience to musician and back again

Yeah, by the end of the night he'd be exhausted, sweaty, wrung out. But he'd also be wired, jazzed, and ready to go for another set or three.

He always left the Thursday night show practically vibrating with energy, wishing he had some way to burn it off.

And tonight, that energy was ramping up even earlier than usual.

He checked his watch and turned to nod at the rest of the band. Counting out the beats, he swung around to face the gathered crowd and began to play.

The sax player was going to be the death of him.

James shifted in his seat, unable to do much about his hard-on other than try to keep it hidden by the table and overall darkness of the club.

Still, it was crowded. And hot. And his khakis weren't quite baggy enough to hide the evidence.

Whatever. It wasn't like he showed up week after week to watch Hot Guy With Saxophone because it did nothing for him.

But Jesus, he was on fire tonight, playing that horn like he was born to it.

Maybe he had been.

The music was quintessentially New Orleans, a blend of jazz and blues with a measure of down-and-dirty rock mixed in. The drummer and the guitarist were both fantastic musicians—they'd have to be, to keep up with the sax player—but he was undeniably the star of the show. Bending low over his horn, then leaning back as he pushed the music up, up, up, he drew all eyes in the club. The songs segued into each other, pulling the crowd along with them, until half the place was on their feet dancing.

Finally, the music stopped, and James sat back in his chair, utterly wrung out. Even seated, his blood was pounding in his veins, his heart thumping to the drum beat that had temporarily disappeared.

Disappointed, he checked his watch, not really surprised to realize that enough time had passed for this to be a logical stopping point for the first set. It always worked like this, the crowd getting so caught up in the music that they could hardly believe it was an hour later already.

Some generic blues tune started blaring over the sound system as the band took a well-deserved break. The people that had been crowding the dance floor turned en masse to the bar, pushing forward to shout their orders to the still-cheerful bartender.

James tipped his chair back against the wall and watched. He was really good at watching. Especially when it came to watching the band, even when they weren't playing.

The sax player set his instrument onto a stand set to the side of the stage and picked up a gaudily-decorated coffee can. He leaned into the mic and shouted, "If you're liking the music tonight, we won't turn down a tip or two. And if you aren't having a good time, you'd better think about your life choices." Grinning, he hopped the short distance off the stage and started weaving his way through the crowd.

Women in miniskirts dug in tiny purses for bills to toss in the can. Guys opened their wallets to add a few dollars as the sax player passed by. The fuchsia-wigged bridal party pooled their cash and shoved it into the bride's hands, urging her forward with catcalls and raucous laughter. She wiggled the wad of bills in front of the sax player's face. In response, he wrapped his free arm around her waist, dipped her low, and planted a kiss on her bright red lips.

When he brought her upright again, there was a smear of red on his lips, accentuating his even white teeth.

He was grinning down at her as the crowd hollered for more. She was still clinging to his shoulders with one hand and holding her wig and tiara on her head with the other. He leaned down and said something to her that had her dissolving in laughter, and he took the opportunity to spin her gracefully out of his embrace. Then he moved on, twisting and turning his way through the raucous bar crowd.

James leaned forward, elbows propped on the tabletop, and watched avidly. The man's hips swayed ever so slightly in time with the music, drawing the eye to the waist and below. Not that James wouldn't be checking him out in that general area anyway. The faded denim clung in all the right places, accentuating his...assets...even in the dim light of the bar.

With a start, James realized that the man was actually heading toward the far wall of the building, almost directly to where he was sitting.

This was unusual. In all the months he'd been coming to the Thursday show, none of the musicians or their crew went much beyond the bulk of the crowd, preferring to stay nearer the bar or dance floor where most of the customers congregated. James usually just dropped a twenty in the tip jar on his way out the door.

But tonight, the object of his lust was walking right towards him.

Half-standing, he fumbled in his back pocket for his wallet, never taking his eyes off the sax player.

He managed to pull a bill out right as the man himself stopped next to his chair.

He reached up and dropped his twenty in the decorated chicory can.

There was a long, slow pause as the sax player looked from the can, to James, and back again. His face impassive, he finally said, "Thanks, *boo*," and turned to walk away.

Holy hell. James slumped back in his chair, blowing out a long, drawn-out breath. The guy was taller than he appeared on stage. That close, James could see the fine stubble on his jawline, blending into the close-cropped goatee. Every inch of him looked totally lickable. And that voice...

Scrubbing a hand through his hair, James watched his fantasy weave through the crowd back to the stage, the faded jeans clinging to his ass like an embrace.

He was going to remember this night for a long, long time.

James stood and wound his way through the crowd to the bathroom. The second set was almost over, and he wanted to beat the rush. Besides, the piano player took the lead on this song anyway.

Despite his best intentions, and the fact that the bar crowd was seventy-five percent female, there was still a line for the men's room, so he queued up and waited for his turn. He waited patiently, only checking his watch twice as he stood there.

Finally, it was his turn, so he went in, turning to close and lock the door behind him. But before he could manage it, someone else pushed his way inside.

"Excuse me," he said, turning to look at the intruder. "I was here first..."

His voice died out. What the hell was *he* doing in here?

The sax player locked the door and turned to James. "*Excuse-moi.*"

His voice was deep, rough, with a little spice tossed in. His Cajun was rich and true, and somehow he made it sound intimate instead of intimidating.

"I could...wait outside..." James fumbled for the door handle, completely out of his depth here. Why hadn't the man cut in line *before* he'd made it inside the bathroom?

"Now why would you want to do that, *cher*, when you're the reason I'm in here in the first place?"

James blinked. Twice.

"Do you think I haven't noticed?" The man stalked forward a few steps, all fluid grace and menacing beauty. "You're here, week after week, always in the same spot, always watching. Watching me."

"I, uh, love your music. The band is fantastic, and the club is very welcoming," James babbled, heart racing, but the other man was already shaking his head.

"I don't think that's it," he murmured, placing his hand flat against the door, right over James' left shoulder. He leaned in, his cheek almost brushing James' as he whispered in his ear. "I think you're here for me."

Oh God. Oh God, oh god, oh *God*. "I'm so sorry. I didn't mean to make you uncomfortable. I'll just—"

The other man cut him off. "My name," he said, "Is Breaux. B-R-E-A-U-X. And I think we need to finish this conversation after the show."

"No, that's okay. I should leave, anyway."

Breaux shook his head slowly, a smile teasing at the corner of his mouth. "Now, that would be a damn shame, you being my biggest fan and all." He leaned in again. "Later."

Then he reached behind James and unlocked the door, pulling it open so he could slip out of the bathroom and disappear into the impatient crowd.

James stood just inside the room, adrenaline coursing through his body, until the next guy in line pounded impatiently on the door and hollered at him to hurry the hell up.

The crowd was starting to filter out of the club as James approached the bar. He needed to pay his tab and get the hell out of here as soon as possible.

Unfortunately, circumstances conspired against him, as the bridal party milled around the bar, blocking his way forward, and the bartender settled bills with everyone except him. He glanced over at the stage, again and again, watching Breaux disassemble and put away his saxophone.

The man was surrounded by gorgeous women in tiny skirts and tinier tops, chattering away about the show and how his playing moved them, truly.

Any other night, James would have rolled his eyes. But tonight, he was too nervous to care.

Breaux had noticed him sitting in the club, week after week. Breaux had approached him. And now he wanted to "finish" the conversation?

No, sir. He was a gay man. He knew how those conversations could go down.

He was going to pay his damn tab, sneak out while Breaux was otherwise occupied, and find another spot to hang out on Thursday nights.

Maybe his living room. That should be relatively safe.

It was too bad, though. He'd enjoyed his evenings here.

"Hey, gorgeous," the bartender said, turning to him. "What can I do for you?"

"Just the bill," he said. "I have to get going."

"Aw, that's too bad." She winked at him. "Sure you don't want to stick around for the after party?"

"Thanks, but I'll pass." He looked at the stage.

Breaux was still busy. "Better get a move on."

"If you're sure." She took his debit card and walked over to the register. "You're practically an honorary employee by this point. You're here enough."

He could feel his face burning. Why the hell had he been so obvious? "Just like the music. And the setting, of course."

"Of course." She tapped a few keys on the register, frowned at it, then tapped a couple more. "And the devastatingly awesome bartender, right?"

"Absolutely." He couldn't be quite sure if she was flirting with him or not. But he was definitely sure that she was taking forever to finish this transaction. If she didn't hurry up, the band was going to be finished and—

"Thanks, *cher*."

James hadn't even noticed Breaux coming up behind him until that moment. The taller, broader man reached over James' shoulder and fist-bumped the bartender.

"You owe me," she grumbled, handing James his debit card with a sheepish smile. "I had to pull every trick in the book to keep him here until you were done."

"Don't worry. I always pay my debts." Breaux stepped to James' side and tilted his head. "You weren't planning on running out on me, were you, *boo*?"

"No, I—"

Breaux leaned in and whispered, "Liar." Then he wrapped a warm, wide palm around James' wrist and tugged him away from the bar.

James looked around. The place was almost empty now, the rest of the band starting to haul their equipment out the front door.

"You gonna help, Breaux?" The keyboardist was standing next to the doorway, a cardboard box in his hands.

"Not tonight," Breaux replied. "I have plans."

In response, the keyboardist just rolled his eyes and walked out the door.

Breaux headed in the opposite direction, pulling a reluctant James behind him.

He should have skipped out on the tab, left a fifty on the table, settled up before the last song. What Voodoo was this man practicing on him, to make him so careless?

The hall outside the kitchen was empty now, a faint rattle of dishes being cleaned echoing out the far doorway. Breaux leaned back against the wall, legs braced wide, still holding James' wrist captive in his hand.

"So, Businessman, you know my name. How about you return the favor and tell me yours?"

Businessman?

"Uh, James. My name is James. But I'm not a businessman."

Breaux flicked the collar of James' button down shirt. "Sure 'nough could have fooled me."

"Look, I'm sorry if I made you uncomfortable earlier—"

Breaux cut him off. "I saw you watching me."

James clamped his mouth shut.

"And I have only one question."

James swallowed.

Breaux tugged James forward until he was standing right between Breaux's legs. "Do you like what you see?"

James felt like he'd swallowed his own tongue. Glancing to the left and right, he could see the hall was still deserted. The noises coming from the kitchen, and out in the main area of the bar, reassured him that there were still people around. Just in case.

Oh, what the hell. He nodded.

To his surprise, Breaux didn't react angrily. Instead, he slid his fingers from James' collar down to the top button of his Oxford shirt. Toying with it, he murmured, "Just like a present, all buttoned up and waiting for me to unwrap it."

Wait, *what*?

"So tell me, *cher*, do you want to be unwrapped?"

"I...I don't understand."

Breaux sighed. He clearly had to be more direct. Leaning down, he captured James' mouth with his.

The man stood there, frozen. Breaux stroked his tongue along the seam of his mouth, and on a gasp, dove right in.

James surged forward, wrapping one arm around Breaux's neck and holding him in place, his tongue chasing Breaux's. He kissed up Breaux's jawline, the smooth shaven skin of James' cheek brushing up against Breaux's stubble, making them both shiver.

Breaux slipped the button out of the buttonhole, exposing a patch of skin at the base of James' neck.

Placing wet, open-mouthed kisses down James' neck, he picked a sweet spot and latched on, licking and sucking the sensitive skin. Then he took James' hand, still held in his grasp, and brought it right down to his hard cock, pressing against the front of his jeans.

"You do this to me," Breaux whispered harshly, his voice in counterpoint to James' panting breaths. "Every week, watching me. With your proper looks and your hungry eyes. What do I do to you?"

He slid his other hand around James' back, curving over his khaki-covered ass, and urged him silently forward until their bodies aligned.

They both groaned, voices echoing in the empty

hallway, separated only by the clothing they wore and the grip of James' hand. The press and the friction, the naughty thrill of being somewhere they could be caught at any moment, had Breaux on the edge within seconds. Reluctantly, he pulled away, gratified when James chased after his mouth to give him one more long, deep, wet, dirty kiss, his fingers still stroking the front of Breaux's jeans.

"Much as I'd like to continue this now, *cher*, I'd rather not come in my pants on the first date. So how about heading out? We can...get to know each other."

The man who'd been grinding into him moments ago actually blushed at that. Damn, he was an interesting mixture of buttoned up and ready to ride. Breaux was looking forward to peeling back the layers.

"So, James," he said, tucking his fingers in the man's back pocket as he steered him toward the exit door. "How do you feel about *beignets* for breakfast?"

Want to read more of the

Nine Naughty Novelists?

You're in luck!

(Note: Bring your sense of

humor...)

Vampires! Werewolves! Puppies!
Blood, Boobs and Bimbos!

Theirs was a love that nature never intended. Bigger than Texas. Hotter than Hades. Weirder than...a lot of other things you might have read about up until now.

Self-made zillionaire Rock Fangsworthy is your typical Texas cowboy...well, sort of. Typical in that the only thing this lethally sexy lady-charmer with the hair trigger temper loves more than his horse is his ranch, The Double Fang. Or maybe his boots. Less typical in the fact he's also a four hundred year old vampire with a shocking secret— he can't stand the sight of blood.

Buffi Van Pelt is just your average girl-next-door winery owner...or is she? The spunky single mom to twin boys also happens to be a winsome werewolf with secrets and troubles of her own. The winery that the gutsy good-girl recently inherited from her grandmother is on the verge of ruin. If Buffi can't find a use for the mysteriously tainted wine before time and her pantry's limited supply of red meat runs out, she and her pups will be left homeless, destitute and very, very hungry. Worse yet, her baby-daddy is the same hunky, bad-boy vampire rancher who's out to steal The Best Little Winery in Bloodsuck from under her paws.

Once upon a time their passion flamed hotter'n a summer's night in Dallas with three Cheerleaders and a side of habanero sauce. Tonight, love's lightning might just strike them twice...but only if the wine don't kill them first.

Turn the page to read the first chapter....

The Zillionaire Vampire Cowboy's Secret Werewolf Babies

Chapter One

It was a dark and stormy night in Bloodsuck, Texas—the kind of night vampire cowboy Rock Fangsworthy loved best. All except for the stormy part. Too much rain made the brim of his Stetson go limp. And if there was one thing Rock wasn't, it was limp. He was rock hard, through and through, from the flinty gaze in his slate-blue eyes to the diamond-tipped spurs on his custom-made, hand-crafted Lucchese lizard skin boots. In fact, Rock had only one soft spot, and that was for his ranch, the Double Fang.

The ranch had been in his possession for several generations, ever since he'd fled Boston at the turn of the last-century-plus-one hoping to leave his family's nest, his disgrace, and the truth about his shameful condition behind and start life anew in that paradise on Earth known as the Texas Hill Country.

The Double Fang occupied some of the prettiest country in all of Texas, *ergo* the world. And as Rock rode across it tonight, he was filled to overflowing with feelings of contentment and self-satisfaction—even despite the rain and the currently questionable condition of his hat. He was master of all he surveyed. There was, in fact, only one thing marring his happiness; one burr beneath his saddle, so to speak; one blot on his otherwise blot-free horizon.

The Best Little Winery in Bloodsuck.

Rock's jaw clenched at the thought. A vein in his temple began to throb. "Grape farmers," he growled, even though there was no one to hear him but his horse, Monk. "No good, double-crossing werewolf scum."

Rock had no use for wineries. After all, he didn't drink...wine. He had no use for werewolves either, not since the day the Braveheart brothers, Butch and Barkley, had cheated him out of a prime parcel of land that should, by rights, have belonged to him. The pair had caught him napping during the day (an unfortunate necessity for those of his kind) and took the opportunity to mark their territory—not just in the manner of wolves, which would have been bad enough, but with stakes and flags and deed contracts—the kinds of thing the County Assessor's Office put such child-like faith in.

Rock had tried twice to right the terrible wrong that had been done him, but both times he'd failed. His last attempt had been made shortly after Barkley, the second of the brothers to die, was killed in a routine hunting accident. He'd approached the widow Braveheart with his offer to buy her out, but had been rebuffed. Babs Braveheart might have been beautiful, but she had the brains to match her blonde good looks and was crazy to boot. She'd taken it into her head that Rock was at fault for her husband's death.

Like anyone could be reasonably expected to distinguish between one wolf and another at a distance of several feet!

Babs had taken her revenge on Rock, sure enough. She'd made certain he didn't get the only two things he'd ever wanted. But now the ding-dong bitch was dead, God rest her spiteful soul. Tonight, he would make his third and final offer for the winery. An offer the new owner, whoever he was, would not be able to refuse.

Rock reined his horse to a stop in the winery's front yard and dismounted. He tied Monk to a conveniently placed grape arbor, a landscape feature that evoked sweet memories of better times. The vein in his temple throbbed harder. That arbor would be the first thing he'd have dismantled once the winery was his. He smiled as he imagined herds of happy cows frolicking in the vineyards, trampling the grapes, the tender fruit turning to jelly beneath their hooves.

His spurs jingle jangle jingled in a pleasantly menacing fashion as he strode confidently up to the front door. High pitched barking noises emanated from inside the house. Rock sneered at the sound. It pleased him to think the former werewolf home now housed a passel of pocketbook dogs, even though they'd shortly be gone as well.

Just as he was about to pound commandingly on the door, it was thrown open.

Rock stiffened. His jaw clenched harder. His vein throbbed. Again. "Buffi Van Pelt. I should have known you'd be back." But, really, how could he have known something like that? Who would ever have expected that Babs and Barkley Braveheart's granddaughter would return to the scene of their crime of passion? An awful suspicion took hold in his mind. "Don't tell me *you're* the new owner of The Best Little Winery in Bloodsuck?"

"Well, of course I'm the new owner," she answered in flustered tones. She seemed distracted by the two puppies gamboling about at her feet. "What did you expect?"

Rock ignored her question—and the puppies. As his gaze roved over the lithe yet athletic form of the woman he'd once been foolish enough to think he might love, the years since he'd last seen her (five, at least, wasn't it? he was almost certain it had been that long) melted away as though it had been no more than two years. Three years, tops. He took note of her strong calves, her breasts rising and falling beneath the thin t-shirt she wore, her rosy cheeks, her red lips.

Her eyes were still as blue as Texas bluebonnets. And her hair—oh, how he remembered that glossy, gold mane, so similar in color and texture to the coat of the golden retriever puppy he'd loved as a child.

He'd named the puppy Rosebud. It had been his faithful companion for three-quarters of an afternoon. Until his cousin Viggo decided to eat him for a snack. Rock could still recall the sick horror he'd felt when he'd come upon them in the kitchen that day; Viggo's mouth stained red with Rosebud's blood, the puppy's lifeless body hanging limp in his hands...

A sharp tug on his ankle brought Rock's mind back to the present. He looked down. Way down. Down to where the two puppies—wolf-hybrids obviously, not pocketbook dogs after all, nor Golden Retrievers either, more's the pity—were viciously attacking one of his custom-made, hand-crafted Lucchese lizard skin boots with the diamond-tipped spurs.

"Shoo," he said as, gently but with firmness, he kicked his foot in an effort to dislodge the pests.

Buffi clapped her hands. "Vlad! Ivan! Stop that this minute!" she scolded.

Rock stared at her in disbelief. She'd named her dogs after his father and grandfather? Oh, the fickle cruelty of women! Why did she not just stake him through the heart and have done with it? The vein in his temple throbbed its agreement.

Rock Fangsworthy. Buffi stared at the familiar yet almost forgotten hard, chiseled features of the man who'd won her heart and taken her virginity. She still could not believe he was here. Out of all the wineries in all the towns in all of Texas, he'd walked into hers.

"What do you want from me, Rock?" she asked. She was terrified she knew the answer, but how? How could Rock have possibly found out he was Vlad and Ivan's father? Who could have told him? Surely not her grandmother! Why, Babs had hated Rock. She'd hated him as much as she'd hated grape rot, powdery mildew and glassy-winged sharpshooters all put together!

"I'm here to buy the winery, of course," Rock answered. His words were like silver bullets, each one aimed straight at her poor broken heart. The very same heart she'd only recently finished painstakingly piecing back together. Buffi was not surprised when the overly abused organ crumbled to bits once more, falling apart like so much overcooked liver. Her grandmother had been right. Rock had used her. He'd toyed with her affections. The winery was all he'd ever really wanted from her. All he ever would want.

"Well, you can't have it, Rock. Do you hear me? The Best Little Winery in Bloodsuck is not for sale!"

Rock's jaw clenched. The vein in his temple started to throb. Buffi was reminded of those magical nights they'd spent in her grandmother's grape arbor. She remembered the passion they'd shared, Rock's hard, throbbing body, his gravel-voiced excitement and her own enthusiastic licking of his face.

Damn you, Rock Fangsworthy. Damn you to hell!

"I think you should leave now, Rock," Buffi said coldly. "There's nothing here for you anymore."

"This isn't over, Buffi," Rock promised. "You haven't seen the last of me."

"Oh, I think I have, Rock," Buffi rejoined as she slammed the door in her baby-daddy's face. "I really think

I have!"

HERE'S WHAT READERS HAVE SAID ABOUT THE *ZILLIONAIRE VAMPIRE COWBOY'S SECRET WEREWOLF BABIES:*

Rhonda Valverde:

If you're looking for a good story to lighten your mood and make you laugh out loud, then you need to pick up The Zillionaire Vampire Cowboy's Secret Werewolf Babies! You'll love the way these characters interact with each other.

Deborah E. Ehling:

The humor starts from the first sentence and continues until the last sentence and feels like one voice wrote the story. It was obvious that the authors had fun with this story, from the character and place names to the cliches....but I laughed all the way through! If you need a lighthearted, lift your spirits, laugh till you can't breathe story, you will enjoy every part of this one!

Someone Who Was Very Confused:

This book was terribly dry and not funny in any way. I expected to laugh as much as I did with Yours, Mine and Ours and it's prequel "The Nanny Years". This book was a complete waste of time and although it was promising it never delivered. I have to question if I was even reading the same book as all these other reviewers that raved, were they paid in advance?!

Pirates! Ninjas!
Secret twins
Pseudonyms!
(Not to mention the parrot, the ferret
and the alligator...)

Being a Tale of Panting Passion wherein a Disaffected Duke runs away to Sea to become a Pirate and ends up becoming Love Slave to a Ninja Queen, whilst at home he is replaced by a Nefarious Highwayman and ne'er-do-well who is, in turn, Ultimately Redeemed by his love for a Poor but Virtuous Governess...

Turn the page to read the first chapter...

If You Give a Duke a Duchy
or
Love's Savage Whiplash
(Not Your Typical Regency Romance)

Chapter One
The Importance of Being Ornithological:
In which a Disastrous Failure to Communicate occurs, resulting in a young Peer of the Realm suffering a Sudden and Egregious Change of Station

Netherloin Park, seat of His Grace, the Duke of Earl, twenty years previously…

The Ninth Duke of Earl was most decidedly not having a good day. Despite its being the fifth anniversary of his birth, at present that esteemed young gentleman could be found lying stretched fully out upon the floor of his bedchamber drumming his feet against the boards and loudly bemoaning his fate.

Fate, in the person of his valet—and the loathsome flowered silk waistcoat that the Duke had been given to understand must be put on, *tout de suite*, if he ever wished to be allowed to join his twin brother for tea—was unmoved by the Duke's distress. A dour Frenchman who went by the name of Lumière, the Duke's valet was mostly deaf and possessed of very little English and was thus largely unmindful of the vulgar imprecations currently being flung at his head by his young charge. To be called a jingle-brained, chuckleheaded fatwit meant less than nothing to Monsieur Lumière.

"I demand to be told the reason for this bloody racket," the Duke's uncle insisted, appearing at the doorway in a state of slight déshabillé. As usual, his arrival exerted a strange effect on the Duke's pet parrot, Pemberley, a venerable, lavender coloured creature who'd been passed on to the current Duke, along with his title, his valet, and sundry items, on the occasion of his father's demise.

"Murderer! Murderer!" the bird repeated, squawking loudly. It was a call he gave only when in the presence of the Duke's uncle and guardian, the Honorable Mr. Willoughby Wickham the Fourteenth, and only since the death (under somewhat mysterious circumstances) of Mr. Wickham's sister and brother-in-law, the late Duke and his lady.

Sadly, this most curious behaviour on the part of the bird had, as of yet, completely failed to excite the interest of any member of the Duke's family. Had it been otherwise, we might have had a far different story to tell.

Undeterred by the parrot's outburst, and determined to be heard above the bedlam, Mr. Wickham bellowed louder. "Lumière! What is the meaning of this noise?"

"It is Monsieur le Duc," Lumière answered in measured tones, disdaining to raise his voice in so ill-bred a fashion. However, to illustrate his point, he gestured at the boy, still lying prone upon the floor, even though it seemed impossible to imagine that his uncle could have missed either seeing or hearing him. "'e eez refusing to stand up so that I may aseest him in donning 'iz new waistcoat."

"Well, if he won't stand up then pick him up off the floor yourself and put the bloody garment on him! I want my tea and I don't wish to have it held up any longer."

"Tres bien," Lumière replied, sighing resignedly. Already he was envisioning the punishment his tender shins were sure to receive from the Duke's vicious little heels. "Eef you inseest."

"I do inseest. Er, I mean, insist." Somewhat flustered, but confident that his orders would be obeyed forthwith, Mr. Wickham turned to leave the room. The jeers and catcalls of the parrot, still ringing in his ears, brought him back again. "And, Lumière, when you've finished here, do something with that blasted duck!"

"Qu'est-ce que c'est?" Lumière replied in somewhat justifiable confusion. "Do something with le Duc?" While it was true the valet understood only a modicum of English, he certainly could tell the difference between a parrot and a duck. The latter was frequently delightful when served *a l'orange*. The former was, culinarily speaking, neither *comme il faut* nor *a la mode*.

Unfortunately, the honorable Mr. Wickham was a product of a first-rate public school education. As such, while he knew quite a bit about a variety of subjects— notably horse racing, ballroom dancing and how to cheat at cards—he knew next to nothing about most others, ornithology included. As far as he was concerned, one bird was the same as the next; jolly good fun to hunt, but of no earthly use whatsoever otherwise. And certainly not the sort of thing one expected to find in a proper gentleman's bedchamber.

"What more do you wish me to do with 'eem?" Lumière inquired, feeling very much ill-used. He had time off coming to him this afternoon and plans involving one of the upstairs chambermaids, a carpet beater and a length of rope.

"Toss him in the river," came the answer. "I dare say a nice swim is just the thing to put the creature in better humour. Just see that he's removed from this house before the hour is out."

"Nom d'un nom d'un nom," Lumière muttered, as Frenchmen of his station were wont to do, though not a one of them could likely tell you what the expression was supposed to mean. "Toss le Duc into zee rivair?"

All in all, it seemed a very odd request for the young man's guardian to be making, but what could one expect of the English who were, after all, a savage and unmannered race. Perhaps the exercise was intended to effect an improvement on the Duke's moods? Lumière supposed anything that would reduce the boy's lamentable propensity for throwing tantrums was worth a try.

And so it was that the Duke soon found himself bundled in his warmest clothes (in deference to the unseasonably cool weather) being dragged across the lawn by his manservant. The parrot accompanied them, flying overhead and inexplicably intoning in sepulchral tones, "Nevermore, nevermore."

"Bon voyage," Lumière called as he pushed the child into the swiftly moving water. He watched the Duke's progress from the riverbank until the boy's head bobbed out of sight. "Enjoy your swim, *mon petit*. Take care you don't catch cold."

A short while later, a thoroughly waterlogged boy was pulled dripping from the river several miles from the Duke's estate. "Why, what have we here?" his rescuer, an obvious rakehell, exclaimed, as he crouched in the grass beside the small form. "Speak up. What were you doing in the water?"

The boy lay limply on the cold ground and gazed back at him in silence, too exhausted to speak, or perhaps too frightened; the man's clothing and manner clearly marked him as a dangerous and nefarious highwayman.

"Do you not have a name then, boy?"

"Duke of Earl!" a large, lavender parrot called from the branch of an overhanging tree. "Duke, duke, duke of Earl." But, as was usual, the bird was completely ignored.

"So, you're a mute, are you?" The highwayman gazed thoughtfully at the boy, noting that his clothing was of exceptionally good quality and cut. It should bring in a pretty penny when sold. "Oh, well, I suppose there's no harm in that. Children should be seen and not heard in any event, so your silence does not signify in the slightest. I have not the patience to deal with rattle-pates and gabsters anyway. As it happens, I need a quiet, well-behaved servant boy to do my bidding. I imagine you'll serve quite nicely in that regard. I shall call you Westley."

"But my name's not Westley," the Duke (for it was indeed he) exclaimed, finally finding his voice. "And if you please, sir, I'm not a servant, I'm a duke."

The highwayman smirked, not believing the boy for an instant. "Are you really? How splendid!" Standing, he executed a deep bow. "I am, of course, honored to meet you, Your Grace. But, as to the other matter, I'm afraid you've not much choice. I've saved your life, you see. Therefore, whatever you were before, you belong to me now. So, enough of this lazing about. Come along. We've a coach to rob."

"You're a highwayman, aren't you?" the boy asked excitedly as he, too, climbed to his feet. "Am I to be one as well?"

"Indeed you are. For I am the Dread Highwayman Roberts and you, if you live long enough, may one day take my place."

The boy fell silent for a moment as he turned the idea over in his head. "May I still keep the parrot?"

"What, that old thing?" The highwayman gazed

critically at the bird, wondering what price it might bring. "Does it have much life left in it?"

"I shouldn't think so," answered the Duke. "It's been in the family for ever so long. Ages, really."

"And does it know to keep quiet when you tell it to?"

"Not hardly. He squawks all the time, particularly when my uncle's about."

The highwayman smiled. "Then it wouldn't be a very good pet for a highwayman to keep, now would it? Besides, only pirates have parrots—everyone knows that. But if you're a good lad and do as you're told, perhaps I'll get you a ferret one day. How'd you like that?"

The duke shrugged. "I don't know. Never had a ferret."

"Oh, they're all the crack," the highwayman promised. "Top of the trees, they are, and quite the height of fashion. Best of all, they never tell your secrets."

As one might expect, the honorable Mr. Wickham was a good deal distressed when news of the Duke's disappearance and apparent demise was brought to his attention. Why, for the first half hour or so the gentleman was quite beyond the reach of consolation, his spirits absolutely sunk in the very depths of despair.

After all, he stood to lose not just his nephew, and his position as conservator of the young man's estate (along with a large annual stipend and the prestige that went with said position) but also quite possibly his life, should his part in this regrettable tragedy ever come to light. His deliverance from the worst and most unpleasant of these consequences was due in no small part to his late sister's efficiency in having presented her lord and master with both an heir and a spare at one stroke.

The Duke's twin brother, Colin by name, although he was possessed of a much more amiable temperament, bore a more than passing—indeed, some might even have termed it remarkable—resemblance to his noble sibling. There was, in fact, only one sure method by which the brothers might be told apart and that was by way of the matching birthmarks they displayed on extremely sensitive portions of their anatomy (i.e., upon the left buttock cheek of one brother and the right cheek of the other). It may also be worth noting that when the two boys stood side by side these curious and improbable marks lined up in such a fashion as seemed to present a very rude picture—that of two ducks engaged in illicit congress. Even more remarkable (although, of course, completely unrelated to our tale) is the fact that this very same image also appeared on the ducal crest.

Due to the boys' tender age, they had not yet been presented at Court. It was, therefore, not widely known that the Duchess had given birth to twins. Indeed, it would have been considered quite scandalous to even speak of such matters in Polite Society. And so, as Mr. Wickham was quick to perceive, in his nephew Colin he had the means to effect a most Infamous Switch without anyone ever being the wiser.

To be sure, the knowledge that he was, without doubt, behaving in an ungentlemanlike manner did cause Mr. Wickham a moment's pause. But only the one moment, and then he was over it. Since his duplicity would serve—and quite neatly too, if he did say so himself—to save his aristocratic bacon (to say nothing of his neck!) he chose not to refine upon it overmuch.

And so begins our story.

HERE'S WHAT READERS HAVE SAID ABOUT *IF YOU GIVE A DUKE A DUCHY:*

Hockeyvamp:
Please read the entire book to its completion. It is comic brilliance and the naming of characters and such after famous authors, singers and characters only adds to its charm for me.

Tricia:
They've done it again!   They had me laughing out loud at the "Dear Sir or Madam" letter to readers at the beginning of thse book. Once again these Nine Naughty Novelists have put together a story that had me laughing out loud.

Mandi, aka Smexy at Smexy Books Romance Reviews:
"I really didn't know what to expect when I started this book but I really enjoyed the time I spent reading it. Even though each chapter has a different author, you really couldn't tell. It flows together well, and it made me smile and laugh throughout. As the authors remind you, this is a parody, not meant to be taken seriously, and I think they do a nice job with it. A fun way to spend an afternoon."